MW01240445

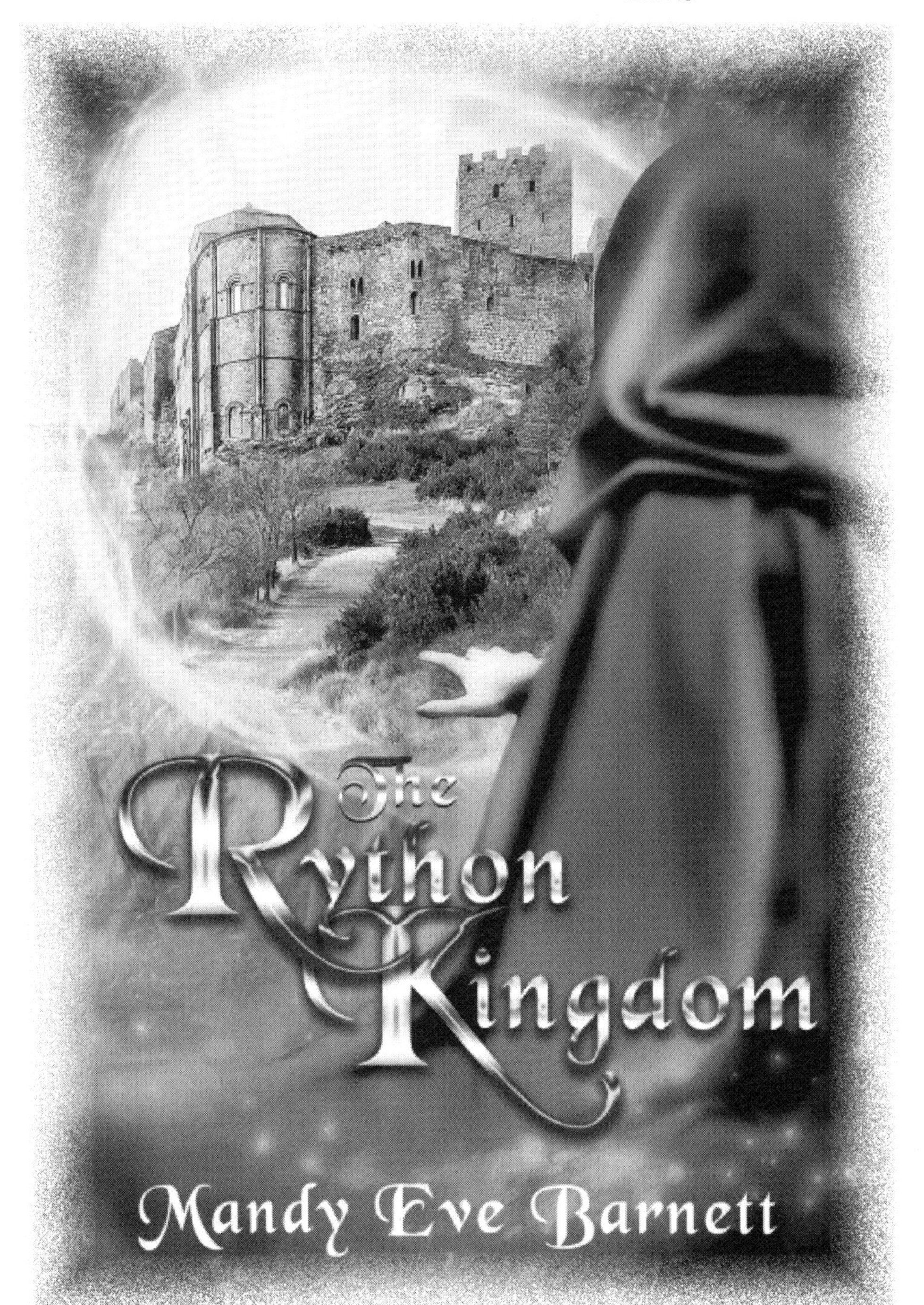
The
Rython
Kingdom
Mandy Eve Barnett

Dream Write Publishing
P.O. Box 57083 RPO Eastgate
Sherwood Park AB Canada
T8A 5L7

www.dreamwritepublishing.ca

The Rython Kingdom

ISBN 978-1-927510-23-0
Cover Design by Winter Bayne (winterbayne.com)

This second edition released by the author contains a new cover design and minor corrections to the text and layout. There are no major changes to the story content.

Library and Archives Canada Cataloging in Publication
The Rython Kingdom
Eve-Barnett, Mandy (b. June 18, 1958)
Sherwood Park AB Canada

Printed in the US by CreateSpace
Also available in E-Book

This book is dedicated to:
My mentor and dearest friend, Linda Pedley,
without her encouragement, support, and expertise
I would not be writing.

Chapter One

"He's coming! He's coming! Guillem Ruet is here!"

Guillem smiled at the group of children running beside his horse as he rode toward the castle's drawbridge. Dirty and barefooted, these youngsters would not be lucky enough to hear his newest tale, first hand. That pleasure would be for the inner court alone. It was a strange and most complex tale and all the more mysterious for being made of a dream.

Shouts of his approach preceded him, thrown from one person to the next across the dirt track and woven amongst the shacks lining it. The summer heat had denuded the earth of moisture; dust swirled around his mount's hooves, creating a cloak of fine grains behind them, shrouding rider and horse. Ahead, the King's standards lay limp against their poles high above on the castle turrets; thin strips of coloured cloth obscuring the lion head emblem of the king. More children, and some adults, ran beside him, eager to witness this famed troubadour first hand. The talk among the courtiers and peasants alike had been of his arrival and little else for many weeks.

As Guillem entered under the portcullis, it brought back memories of returning from battle years previously. Conquering heroes were showered with flowers and rewarded with grand feasts and warmed by many a maid. Serving as a knight in his younger days, Guillem had been admired for his prowess in battle, but now he was even more revered as a troubadour. His tales of battles and faraway lands held audiences spell bound as he punctuated them with displays of swordsmanship and the exhibiting of combat scars. So popular was Guillem that a feast or festival without his presence was considered incomplete. Fierce competition between lords kept Guillem's purse and belly full as he travelled from one borough to the next, shamelessly attending whomever paid the highest fee. His new life fulfilled his wander-lust. Being confined to one place filled him with dread as did faithfulness to just one maid. Why restrict yourself to one when there were so many to pick from—all willing to bed the famous knight and troubadour?

Word had reached him a month prior notifying him the king himself requested Guillem's presence at court. It was an honor to be bestowed with such a command and Guillem did not hesitate to comply. Not dallying at Lord Suffolk's seat; as was his usual habit. Normally, he would take advantage of the many benefits afforded him but, this time, he packed his saddlebags the very same night and set off toward the king's domain at daybreak. Several requests for his presence had made it to his ears as he travelled but each was declined in favor of an audience at the king's court. Once it was common knowledge the king had requested Guillem to speak, Guillem knew he would be able to use it to increase his fee.

Ahead of him now was the sovereign's castle keep with sentries standing at both sides of a stairway leading up to massive oak doors. The excited crowd jostled for position to get closer to Guillem and perchance to touch him or his fine mount. A herald sounded his trumpet as Guillem dismounted. The shouts died away as all eyes centered on the keep's immense doors. They slowly opened. All knees bent and heads bowed as the regal figure of King Henry was revealed, resplendent in deep purple robe and golden crown. With measured steps, King Henry descended the stone stairs.

"Welcome, Guillem Ruet, your reputation precedes you. My courtiers and subjects have talked of little else but your arrival for these many weeks. Come and drink ale with me. You must be weary from your journey."

Guillem bowed deeply again then handed his horse's reins to a saddle hand, who was fidgeting beside him. As the boy led his mount away, Guillem could hear the lad's excited whisper to the surrounding crowd.

"Look, look, I have his horse to care for."

Careful to remain a step behind, Guillem followed his King into the castle's dark interior. The huge stone blocks prevented the heat of the outside world from entering. Guillem shivered involuntarily. *I should have taken my cloak out of the saddlebag before releasing my horse into the care of the boy.* Then another thought struck him and he turned to see his horse being led away on the far side of the courtyard—he had not secured the small box. He had promised the mysterious old man he would not let it leave his possession and now it was in the hands of a young stable lad.

"The fire will warm your bones, Guillem. Is something amiss? You seem anxious?"

"Thank you, Sire. I relinquished my cloak without thinking but I also forgot to retrieve a certain object."

"Do not worry, Guillem. I will have your saddlebags brought to your room presently. If there is anything missing I shall deal with the culprit myself. But for now...." The King raised a hand to summon a serf, "Stephen, a robe for our guest."

A young man appeared from the shadow of a stone column and presented Guillem with a thick woolen robe. Its heavy warmth felt pleasing. Serfs opened an inner door as the King approached and allowed the two men to enter the great hall. Long oak tables flanked the centre aisle below a raised platform where the King's ornately carved table and throne stood. Following his sovereign's lead, Guillem walked toward the roaring fire at the far side of the huge room. Its radiant heat was welcome in the cool interior of the castle.

"Sit with me, Guillem, you will soon warm. Bring ale, Stephen."

"As you command, your majesty."

The serf had moved so silently that Guillem jumped when he responded to his master's command.

"Guillem, why do you start so?"

"Sorry, Sire—I was unaware of your serf's presence; gave me a bit of a shock when he spoke."

"Not so surprising, Guillem, we call him Silent Stephen. He seems to glide instead of walk, although to watch him you cannot see any difference from any other man's stride."

"Strange indeed, my Lord, is he born of a witch?"

"Actually no, Guillem, his mother was a maid to my mother. He has grown up within these walls and knows no other life than to live and serve here."

Stephen returned with a large pewter jug and two tankards and set them before the King. He poured a small amount of the golden liquid into a small cup and drank it. After a moment to determine the fluid was not poisoned or tainted, he filled the two tankards, bowed and glided backwards into the shadows. The King laughed at Guillem's obvious puzzlement as he witnessed his visitor's transfixed look by this motion.

"You saw for yourself how he moves, Guillem. Can you explain it?"

"Sire, I am unable to enlighten you or myself as to how he can appear to glide. It is the strangest thing I have seen in many a long year."

"Even with the closet scrutiny my courtiers and I have been unable to fathom his movements."

"I will keep a close eye on him, Sire, while I am a guest in your castle – mysteries are for the solving."

"Well I have been told you have many tales of strange beasts, lands and peoples, Guillem. I look forward to you relaying one or more for me and my court."

"It will be my honor, Sire. I have a new tale to entertain you, as a matter of fact."

"Is it a battle adventure or a horrendous beast tale?"

"It is actually both, my Lord. The tale is so full of rich intricacies and detail that one evening will not be sufficient to relay it in its full glory. Might I relay some now?"

"Such a tempting proposition, Guillem, but no, I shall wait to hear it in its entirety over the three day feast. For now, it is best you rest. Stephen will take you to your quarters."

Again the serf's presence took Guillem by surprise but he managed to hide it from his Lord and the servant. Although he watched the serf's feet intently, Guillem could not accurately discern how the man's feet did not make a sound on the stone flagged floor. His own footfalls echoed back to him even though he was wearing soft leather shoes.

Guillem was led up a narrow stairway to a small barrack room housing four beds.

"Shall I have company this night, Stephen?"

"No, sire. The King commanded you have the quarters alone. Do you require anything?"

Guillem saw his saddlebags placed on one of the bunks.

"It seems I have everything I need for the moment. Thank you, Stephen. The ale and heat from the fire have made me drowsy after my journey so I will sleep for a while. Please, wake me in an hour so I can make ready for the feast."

"As you command, Sire."

The serf, with a slight bow, closed the heavy oak door with the slightest click of the latch, leaving Guillem standing in his temporary quarters. *There is more to that boy than he is telling or indeed meets the eye.*

Before discarding his breeches and tunic, Guillem opened his saddlebag and felt inside. His fingers touched the small box and his unease dissipated slightly. Then he lay down on the nearest bunk and tried to curb his anxiousness as doubts began to cloud his mind. He had been within two days ride of the sovereignty when qualms about his usual repertoire of tales arose. Guillem worried if his tried and tested tales would be worthy of the King's court. As he succumbed to sleep an image of his earlier campfire appeared. He remembered looking deep into the flames, his eyes transfixed by the flickering orange flames. While semiconscious, he recalled they had turned blue in hue taking him to a far away land. The blue flames rose up, twisting and forming into images of a witch and a horrendous beast. A strange and bewitching but marvelous tale had been revealed to him that night, one he felt sure would delight his majesty.

Guillem only became aware of Stephen's reappearance when the young man shook his shoulder to wake him.

"The feast begins within the hour, Sire."

"I will be down directly. Thank you for your timely awakening."

Dressed in a green brocade tunic and white under shirt with dark brown breeches, Guillem made his way down to the great hall. He heard loud voices and laughter accompanied by the minstrels' music on his approach. As he entered the room, he saw every seat at the long tables occupied with men and women dressed in finery. He stood just inside the room to the right of the entrance and waited to be called. The thud of a staff on stone announced the arrival of King Henry. A silence fell in the hall and all heads bowed as the King walked with his Queen on his arm to the high table. Once he and the queen were seated, the King nodded for his courtiers to resume their merriment. Serfs brought platter after platter of food to the head table as well as numerous pewter jugs. Once the high table was fully laden more servants covered the lower tables with even more platters and jugs. Guillem watched a servant walk toward him after noticing the King speak to the serf.

"The King wishes you to sample the fare before entertaining him. Follow me."

Guillem was escorted to a small table just below the high table where meat, bread and ale were laid out for him. Before he sat down, he nodded his thanks to the King. The bread soaked up the meat juices and he ate heartily but spared the ale. He would need his wits about him when telling this specific tale. As was his custom he usually punctuated his tales with displays of swordsmanship and the exhibiting of combat scars, but this one was different. In all his years serving as a knight and the many as a troubadour, this particular story's origins were a mystery to him. His telling of adventures as a young knight had served him well on many an occasion but this story's depth and detail far exceeded any real battle and accomplishment of his memory.

The feasting courtiers' ruckus filled the great hall for an hour or more. Guillem became anxious as there seemed to be no end to the ale and food. *When would he relay his tale? Surely not when all present are too drunk to enjoy the story?* A sudden thudding demanded attention and the King stood.

"We have feasted well but now we will be entranced with my honored guest, Guillem Ruet. He will recite a new tale for our entertainment—so fill your tankards and let him spellbind us. Please, pray silence for our notorious visitor."

Guillem bowed deeply toward King Henry and Queen Rebecca and stood on one corner of the raised platform.

"Your majesties, lords and ladies, tonight I will entertain you with a story so rich with detail and intrigue you may find yourselves asking for the King's protection this night."

With a slight smile at the transfixed faces before him, Guillem cleared his throat, took one draught of ale and proceeded.

"Picture, if you will; a dark cave in the farthest reaches of an ancient forest. In its depths, a soft glow from flickering flames bathed a young man in its light his vigil, to keep watch for his master. Shadows danced around the young man as he huddled closer to the campfire. Although warmth bathed his face and hands, he still shivered. He wondered how much longer his master would be?

The cavern was cold and damp - water dripping and the crackling fire were the only sounds to keep the young servant company that long night. He listened intently but, alas, could not hear the footsteps that would announce the end of his night's long watch. The light changed, giving a view of the large oak forest beyond the cavern's mouth. Surely, you ask, his master would arrive from the depths soon. His body shivered as a chill ran down his back and he threw a few more sticks onto the fire. But wait; was it only the chill that had him tense? He sensed being watched. The young man jumped to his feet, taking hold of a thick branch as he peered into the gloom.

Guillem was pleased at the sharp intake of breath from his audience but did not pause.

"Do not be afraid, Gideon, it is only me, returning."

"Master, my Lord Elros, you have been gone all night. Are you well, not wounded I trust?"

"I am very well, in fact, better than ever."

"Where are you, Sire, I cannot see you?"

"I am very close but I must tell you not to be afraid before I come into the light."

"Why, Sire, would I be afraid? You are my lord and master."

"My appearance has changed, Gideon, and you may fear the look of me but I assure you I will not hurt you."

The servant, Gideon, took a deep breath and stood facing the darkest part of the cavern's depths. With slight unease, he answered his lord.

"I am ready, Sire, you may show yourself. I am not afraid."

The darkness moved to his left and he turned to face whatever may appear. Golden eyes glinted in the gloom. Gideon was transfixed as a much larger version of Lord Elros, appeared, with muscles bulging and skin the colour of gold. Stunned the servant asked.

"What happened, Sire? Are you cursed?"

"Not cursed, Gideon, I have been blessed by the Rython Griffon. He has bestowed upon me the strength of ten men. I will protect my kingdom from the Horthen beast and the sorceress, Malgraf. This gift will ensure I bring peace to my land."

"My lord, you risked your life to face the Griffon. How did you manage to solve his riddle?"

"My father's seer, Eleanor the Eldest, found parchments deep in the old library which told of a knight named, Correlan. He became very strong after facing the Griffon. The tale of his adventure was written but the answer to the riddle was hidden in secret writing. Eleanor has spent four long years trying to decipher that code on my behalf. Yesterday evening she was successful. That was why I could not wait until the morrow."

"Sire, your appearance will strike fear into many, I am sure, but once they

know it is your intention to save us from the witch and the Horthen, the people will rejoice."

"I trust my Lady Lysse will feel the same, Gideon. Now why are you smiling so?"

"I fear, my lord, that your horse will not be able to carry your increased frame."

At his servant's announcement, Lord Elros, walked to the cavern's entrance and picked up his steed as easily as if it were a goblet. He turned when he heard Gideon giggling at the cave's mouth. In truth, it must have be a strange sight to see a horse carried by a man.

"As you say, Gideon, this poor creature would surely break beneath me. Best we walk back through the forest. I have a duty to do but need to eat a fine feast before I face the Horthen."

Murmuring broke into Guillem's thoughts. The beast had captured his audience's imagination.

"Is this Horthen beast of their realm or another, Guillem?"

"All will be revealed in time…may I continue?"

Guillem witnessed many heads nod accompanied with elbows nudging neighbors. Once silence fell in the hall, Guillem continued.

While the brave lord and his manservant made their way back to the castle. The Lord Elros' lady, Lady Lysse, had been holding her own vigil that very same night, attended by her maidservant, Megan. The attendant although persistent, had been unable to persuade her lady to take to her bed and rest.

"It is late, my lady, you should go to your bed. I will keep watch and promise to wake you when my lord returns."

"I would not sleep, Megan. Knowing he is facing the Griffon fills me with dread. I could not persuade him to send another. I am so fearful."

"My sire is an excellent swordsman, my lady. I am sure he will have no trouble defeating the Griffon."

"May your confidence bode well, Megan. Now please find me a shawl this night air is chilling."

As Megan left her lady's chamber to do her bidding, Lysse knelt and offered a prayer to the High Priestess.

"Priestess, on high, if it is your will, bring my lord back to me unharmed.

His kingdom and I need his protection on this earthy domain."

Lady Lysse became conscious of a pale light across her closed lids and opened her eyes to see a falling star. It truly was a sign from the High Priestess. She would keep Lord Elros from harm. Lysse's heart eased a little and she greeted Megan with a smile upon her return.

"My lady, what has happened?"

"A sign from the High Priestess, herself. My lord will return to us safely, I am sure of it. She let a star fall from her cloak."

"With such a good omen, you would surely sleep now, my lady."

"I may lie upon my bed but to actually sleep, I do not think so. But if I do slip into slumber promise me you will stand vigil, Megan."

"Of course, I will, my Lady Lysse. I will wake you the moment I hear hoof beats in the court yard."

Slumber did not come quickly to the Lady Lysse but eventually she succumbed. Megan wrapped a blanket around her shoulders and sat beside a window overlooking the courtyard. Any sound would surely stir her if she happened to doze. As the soft light of dawn rose from the horizon, Megan's rest was disturbed by hoof beats yonder. Rubbing her eyes she peered into the half-light to see two figures and their mounts enter the courtyard. She went to her lady's bedchamber but hesitated to wake her. She looked so peaceful. Her indecision was interrupted by her master's voice.

"Megan, I will wake my wife – you may go."

The servant did as she was commanded and did not think it strange that her lord spoke from behind the ante chamber doorway.

Whispering among his audience made Guillem smile; gripping them with his storytelling thrilled him. Without pause he proceeded watching all faces before him entranced.

Lord Elros approached his sleeping wife and gently touched her shoulder. With no candlelight to illuminate the dark room, his new form would be concealed, giving him time to help prepare her until he could explain his appearance.

"My love, my Lysse, I have returned to you but I am changed. It is the price I willingly paid for a marvelous gift the Griffon bestowed upon me. Keep your eyes closed until I light a candle."

"As you wish, my love, but why the mystery?"

"I do not want to frighten you. Now you may behold your new husband."

Lysse opened her eyes to see a changed Elros with golden skin and eyes glinting in the half-light of early morn. His sheer bulk took her breath away but she could see his love burning in the yellow eyes that held her to them.

"I have returned to you, my love, with the strength of ten men. I am ready to defeat the Horthen and banish the witch and fear from my kingdom."

"My lord, your appearance does not frighten me, I know you mean me no harm. If your new form will free us of the evil that plagues us, it is a welcomed one. From this day forward I will wear golden cloth to match your magnificent appearance. I love you with all my heart, no matter your shape."

"Lysse, my love, you are truly my queen. I feared you would turn from me."

"Your love shines brightly from within, Elros; it cannot be mistaken."

Elros embraced his wife; his lips felt cool against hers as shadows quivered on the wall. The candles flickered and then fizzled to nothing as the lovers created their own heat.

Guillem took a moment to sip a draught of ale. Couples held hands and gazed into one another's eyes, their thoughts focused on how true love could conquer all. King Henry held up a hand and Stephen bent to hear his command. Guillem watched the young man glide to the far end of the hall and disappear through the massive doors. Again Guillem was intrigued as to how the servant could seemingly float instead of walk. He resolved to further his acquaintance of the eerily quiet servant the following day.

"Please continue, Guillem, I am sure my guests are as anxious as I to hear more of this story."

"As you command, your Highness, it is my pleasure to continue. As you may remember Lady Lysse's handmaiden had been released from her duties and she is the one we shall follow now."

Having taken her leave of Lady Lysse and Sir Elros, Megan made her way back to the servant's quarters. Her eyes burned, with lack of sleep from her night's watch and all she could think of was her bunk and slumber.

"Megan, I must speak with you."

The rasping voice penetrated Megan's sleep deprived mind.

"Eleanor, you scared me. What are you doing awake at this hour?"

"I must speak to you, Megan. Follow me."

"Can it not wait? I have kept watch all night and need to sleep before my lady calls for me again."

"It is the lady I need to speak to you about."

"If you insist, Eleanor, but please be quick, my eyes burn and my body aches."

"Quick is as quick does, Megan. Come this way."

Megan followed Eleanor through the twists and turns of the castle corridors. They eventually arrived at a wooden door. It uttered a loud creak as the old woman pushed it open and walked into darkness.

"Eleanor, where are you taking me?"

"Be patient, Megan, just follow me."

A candle flickered, giving a dim glow to a small room, sparsely furnished. On one side was a bunk and on the other, shelves of books, yellowed with age. Eleanor took Megan's hand and guided her to a stool.

"Our lady may be in danger, Megan. When I unraveled the riddle for Sir Elros, I found out something else. I tried to tell him but he was too impatient to leave."

"What danger is my lady in, Eleanor? What did you find?"

"The riddle is only part of the Horthen curse. Our lady is at risk from the witch Malgraf. She bewitched the beast and it will do her bidding. While Sir Elros is battling the beast, Malgraf will appear as our master and kill Lady Lysse."

Several ladies gasped at Guillem's words but were comforted by their companions enabling him to speak further.

"What can stop the witch, Eleanor?"

"You must ensure our lady wears these."

As the old woman's hand opened, a deep azure beaded bracelet was revealed in her palm. In the depths of the beads, a dancing light was seen within.

"What magic is this, Eleanor?"

"It is powerful magic, Megan, to repel a powerful sorceress. It was the other secret I found with the riddle's answer."

"If these small beads will protect my lady, I will do as you ask, Eleanor."

"Megan, you must deliver these magic beads to our Lady at first light"

"Eleanor, it is first light. I was hoping to sleep for an hour or two before attending to my lady. This day will stretch forever before me."

"I will give you a potion to overcome your tiredness, Megan. Drink it quickly though as it is bitter in taste."

Eleanor handed Megan a small vial containing a thick white substance. The servant put it to her lips and drank the draft as instructed. The liquid's bitterness made her cringe and shiver.

"That is surely the worst thing to ever pass my lips, Eleanor; for that horror I sincerely hope it does keep me awake."

"You will have added vigor and your tiredness will be as if it never existed. Now go to our lady, quickly now."

"I will do as you bid, Eleanor."

A gentle gasp to Guillem's right caught his attention. A fair maid looked up at him with wide eyes.

"Is this Eleanor a witch?"

"She is not a witch of evil intent but a purveyor of potions and wisdom of ages. She has served the Lord Elros and his father before him. Now, shall I continue?"

"Yes, please, forgive me for interrupting."

So Megan left old Eleanor's quarters and made her way back to Lady Lysse's rooms with the blue beads encased in an ornately decorated box. She gently tapped on her mistress' door and waited. She knew not to enter until given permission. Her master, Lord Elros, had been with Lady Lysse when Megan left and it would not do to intrude.

"Come."

The deep voice confirmed Lord Elros was indeed present. Megan bowed deeply as she entered and only when she straightened did she see her master's new form. Uttering an involuntarily a gasp of surprise, she recoiled slightly.

"Ah, Megan, my shape is somewhat changed but my newfound strength will release my kingdom from the Horthen curse."

"Sire, you are indeed changed –your stature is so much larger. I am sure you will have no trouble defeating the beast."

"That is indeed my intention, Megan. Now I am in need of a hearty breakfast. Please send word to the cook forthwith."

"Yes, Sire, I will attend to it but firstly I must present my lady with something Eleanor the Eldest gave me this very morn."

"You have something from Eleanor? Show me."

Megan presented the small box to her master and stood back. Sir Elros opened the lid and gazed at the beaded bracelet."

"These are very fine beads, Megan. What is their purpose?"

Megan looked toward her mistress' bed, anxious not to cause her distress. She whispered.

"Eleanor, found some writings concerning the Horthen curse…."

"Yes, I know that. Did I not solve the riddle and have the Rython's gift bestowed upon me?"

"My lord there was another part to the writings which Eleanor did not have time to tell you."

"Then speak up girl, what detail was I not told?"

"Eleanor discovered the riddle was only part of the Horthen curse. Our lady is at risk from the witch, Malgraf. She has bewitched the beast to do her bidding and while you are in battle she will appear before our lady disguised as you, sir, and slay her."

"We must set guards around my lady at once."

"My lord, Eleanor told me these beads possess a powerful magic and as long as our lady wears them they will protect her from Malgraf."

"Leave us, I will ensure Lady Lysse wears the beads. Go about your duty – my hunger is great."

Elros looked upon the beads once more and then closed the lid. Approaching the bed he gently stroked Lysse's face.

"Wake, my darling, it is the morrow and I have to leave before too long. My journey to find the Horthen must begin this very day."

"Elros, my love, you should have rested longer."

"I wanted to find a treasure for you; something to remind you of me while I travel to far off lands."

"A treasure is not needed, my love I remember your face; your kind hands."

Elros placed the small box in her hand. She looked up in surprise and as the lid opened, her face lit up with wonder.

"They are so beautiful, Elros, as if they have an inner light."

"Promise me you will wear them constantly."

"If that is your wish, my love, I will."

Sighs of wonderment and loving looks between couples in his audience interrupted Guillem's flow. King Henry stilled the murmuring with a raised hand and again nodded for Guillem to continue.

Once Elros was satisfied the beads were safely on Lysse's wrist, he escorted her to the great hall for breakfast. Horrified faces and gasps of shock accompanied them as they walked the corridors. Lysse tried to pacify the young and old with assurances that their Lord was of no threat to them.

"See your Lord's magnificent new form a gift to ensure he is victorious in the battle against the Horthen. Fear not."

Elros held her arm as they walked, his head bowed to hide the golden glint within his eyes. He was sure the strange manifestation would further alarm the household population. It was enough he was doubled in size.

As they entered the hall they saw the high table resplendent with platters of meat, bread and fruit. More servants cringed at the sight of their morphed lord and once again Lysse reassured them he was of no threat. Elros' hunger took some time to be sated with several more platters brought from the kitchens. Once they had time to look upon him, the servants realized his new shape would, indeed, give him an advantage against the beast. Once they were out of ear shot the talk passed from one to another throughout the castle and beyond. In less than a day, several outlining villages would hear the news.

In the grand dining hall, Lord Elros eventually sat back, satisfied much to Lady Lysse' amusement.

"Your appetite is vast, my lord, we will have to have more stock bred for the season."

"Indeed, Lysse. It takes many plates to sate my new form. I will have Captain Sylus send word to the farmers that greater numbers of cattle, sheep, and pigs are required."

"And don't forget extra barrels of ale, my love. You drink as if parched."

Elros' deep laughter echoed in the hall at Lysse's comment. He enjoyed his wife's company and her light humor but he could not delay much longer.

His plan was to travel to the Dark Mountains that very day to find the Horthen and destroy it. For extra protection of his ladylove, he organized guards to be posted day and night around his wife. He meant to succeed in his quest to end the curse's blemish upon his land and to kill the witch Malgraf.

Cheers rang out in support of Lord Elros. It gave Guillem time to partake of a couple of sips of ale as he listened to the comments.

"Truly a heroic man."

"He will surely succeed."

"His bravery is evident."

"Please, carry on Guillem, we must know of the beast's fate."

"Of course, my majesties, lords and ladies, it is my pleasure to continue."

With breakfast concluded, Elros commanded his troops be readied for an arduous journey and plenty of provisions were loaded onto pack mules. He instructed Captain Whitlow to speak in his stead and ask for volunteers for the mission at hand. Elros knew his soldiers were valiant and courageous, but this particular undertaking could mean many would not return. He wanted only those men willing to make the sacrifice to accompany him on this quest. The captain returned word that all were indeed prepared to fight beside their lord, no matter the price. The safety of the kingdom, and those within it, was their ultimate goal.

"The contingent is ready to depart at your word, Lord Elros."

"Thank you, Captain Whitlow I will join you shortly."

Elros turned to Lysse and embraced her, careful to temper his new strength, for fear of crushing her delicate frame.

"Keep to the castle until I return, my love, dangers are more apt to retaliate when faced with destruction."

"I have Captain Sylus and his troop to protect me, Elros, I will be secure."

A lingering kiss; then a touch of her face before leaving would have to satisfy him until his return.

With heavily laden saddlebags and a thick cloak pulled tightly around him, Elros bade farewell one last time to his lady as he mounted a great black Percheron horse—the strongest and largest steed available in the kingdom. Gideon jerked the pack mule's reins and followed his master astride his own mare. As they rode underneath the battlements, Gideon viewed Megan and Eleanor standing in the shadows. Eleanor raised her hand and a blue light flashed towards their master. The light dispersed into a yellow wisp and wrapped around Lord Elros' shoulders. Gideon nodded his thanks as another wisp touched his chest. As the two men rode away, Megan faced Eleanor.

"What spell did you cast, Eleanor?"

"The most potent protection spell I know. We must hope it will be enough. Lord Elros is up against a ferocious beast and a powerful sorceress."

"Surely, with the Griffon's gift and your magic, Lord Elros will succeed?"

"We can but wait for their safe return, Megan."

Eleanor shuffled away into the shadows leaving Megan frowning at her back. She looked back to the courtyard then made her way over to Lady Lysse.

"My lady, please, go back into the warmth before you take a chill."

"Just a while longer, Megan. I will leave when they are on the crest of yonder hill."

The sudden halt in the storytelling had Guillem's audience looking at him expectantly.

"Your majesty, the hour grows late and the tale is but half finished. With your permission, I shall continue tomorrow evening."

"You have us at your mercy, Guillem. I see the moon is whole and bright this night. We shall rejoin Elros and his troop at feast's end tomorrow,"

Then, the King stood, holding a tankard up high.

"Lords and ladies, join me in a show of gratitude to Guillem."

The room was silent for a moment as the audience held up their tankards still lost in the wonders of the tale; then the applause started. Guillem took a bow and then a mouthful of ale as the ovation continued. Tankards thumped on tables and hands clapped enthusiastically. Guillem graciously took bow after bow. The King raised his tankard toward him and nodded, smiling. Guillem knew he had captured them all in his tale and it brought him great joy. He would rest well that night and on the morrow he would seek out Stephen—to solve that particular riddle. As he walked through the great hall, Guillem received numerous congratulations and pats on the back. Questions as to the fate of Elros were asked but he declined to answer.

"Tomorrow night all shall be revealed."

Chapter Two

Once back in his quarters, Guillem was pleasantly surprised to find a fire burning brightly and his bunk warmed with a pan full of hot coals. He was thankful for Stephen's attendance and began to formulate a plan to garner the servant's trust. For now, he would enjoy a deep slumber and rest his voice. His eyes closed and sleep was upon him instantly. Guillem was unaware of a cyan glow beneath his pillow. A thread emitted from a small orb traced across Guillem's eyes—the tale's details entering his mind in dream form. The richness of detail would ensure a captivated audience and the enchantment recited true.

Duties completed, Stephen retired to his small room deep within the castle's depths. A single flame gave out a feeble light as he sat on a wooden bunk. Confident he was quite alone he retrieved an orb from its secret hiding place behind a loose stone in the wall. With his hands cupped around the object, in reverence, he whispered a chant. The swirling cyan mist within gradually cleared and Malgraf's face appeared.

"Mistress, there is something amiss. The troubadour tells a tale of your rule—how can that be?"

"Gentle Stephen, do not fret, it is I who planted the tale into his mind. He will relay the story in all innocence. He is totally unaware of the magic I laid upon him several days ago and also this very night."

"Should I feed him poison or some other draught to halt his telling of the tale?"

"Do not stop or harm the troubadour in any way. He will play his part as I have contrived. His reciting of the enchantment will be without concern—he only sees it as part of the story and nothing more. However, unbeknownst to him he will utter the release spell and free me from my prison. Once I am released I shall deal with those who ensnared me."

"I have waited so long to witness your freedom, my excitement is difficult to contain."

"But contain it you must, Stephen; in a few short hours this kingdom will once again be under my control. King Henry will suffer the punishment of his father's betrayal and audacity to incarcerate me. These are my lands and all will bow before me once again."

Stephen held the orb to his chest, feeling it tingle with encased power. His wait was almost over and then he could discard the ludicrous pretense of mere mortal, once and for all. As he carefully wrapped the precious object in folds of fabric, his eyes glowed turquoise in the candlelight. *Stop—you fool, you must not betray yourself now—keep your true self hidden for a while longer.*

Bird song and sunshine welcomed Guillem as he walked into the castle's inner courtyard. Servants, pageboys, and stable hands were busy at their various tasks and their footfalls echoed on the cobblestones.

"May I be of service, Sire Ruet?"

The young stable hand from the previous day was beside Guillem before he had the chance to survey the whole scene.

"Yes, you may ready my horse. I shall take an early morning ride before breakfast."

"It will be my honor, sire."

"Are you at my service this morrow?"

"If it is your wish, sire I have been instructed to care for your steed and fulfill any other needs you may have without the castle. Stephen is responsible for satisfying your needs within the castle walls."

"Then I find I am in need of your services this morn...your name?"

"Archie, sire."

"Saddle my horse and a mare for yourself, Archie we shall ride out and enjoy this beautiful day."

Guillem smiled at the boy's obvious joy at his command and watched the young lad run to the stables. While he waited he looked around him. The castle walls were made of thick grey stone blocks and signs of age were evident. Moss, lichen and weathered edges of the corner stone's told him the castle stood for many generations. King Henry was the twelfth in a long line of sovereigns to rule the land.

"Your horse is magnificent, Sir Ruet, and so mild in manner."

"I am not in need of a wild and sturdy stallion now-a-days; my fighting days are over so I content myself with a mild mannered mount. He is named Florion."

"He is still a handsome beast."

"Thank you, Archie. Now, shall we ride? You can show me the best trails."

"For a pleasant ride we should go west, sire. The sloping fields rise slowly and atop will give you vast views of his majesty's lands."

"Then that is what we shall do."

From his place in the shadows, Stephen watched Guillem and the boy in discussion and their exit through the ramparts. He would go about his daily duties all the while tempering his excitement for the evening's event. There was no pity in his heart for all the people around him, only the desire to have the power promised to him.

Atop the wheat field, Guillem listened to Archie describe each focal point.

"The plume rising on the next hill is from the smokehouse in a village called Warden. I was born and raised there until I could be of service."

"I sampled some fine smoked meat last night, does it come from Warden?"

"Yes, his majesty favors the Warden meats. To the right you can see the glint of a river and nestled next to it is the hamlet of Storing-on-Lee. Fine cloth is woven and dyed there."

As the sun's warmth bathed them, man and boy discarded their cloaks and wrapped them in rolls on top of the animals' withers so as to hold them as they rode.

"You are an excellent guide, Archie. I have ridden far and wide but have not had the pleasure before of such a knowledgeable young companion."

"Thank you, sire. It is an honor to be of service to such a personage as yourself. Your acts of bravery as a knight and wondrous tales as a troubadour have delighted me many a night."

"Well, what say you to some breakfast? The gurgling of my stomach is now a real distraction."

"It will be my pleasure to escort you to the great hall, sire."

"For your excellent service I shall ensure you are well compensated."

The breeze rushing past their faces was welcomed as they galloped down the hill toward the castle. The full sun promised a heat filled day. The cool interior of the castle would be pleasant as the day wore on, that was certain.

Once inside the castle's keep, Archie took hold of Florian's reins and waited for Guillem to dismount. As he turned toward the stables, Guillem laid a hand gently upon his young shoulder.

"Wait there young man, I do not forget a promise."

Guillem entered the great hall, filled a plate with meat, bread and fruit, and then returned to the courtyard.

"For your services this morning, Archie; I want you to enjoy your very own feast."

Archie looked around him in trepidation.

"Sire, if I am seen with such a plate, I will be punished for thieving."

"I did not think. Wait… I have an idea."

Guillem searched his saddlebag and retrieved a small hessian cloth.

"There, you can wrap your feast within this cloth – mind that no-one takes it from you or they will have me to answer to."

Guillem looked around at several curious faces and announced.

"Archie has been of service to me this morn, I expect no-one to bother or steal from him – this is my gift. If word comes to my ear that he has been released of this fare the culprit will have to answer to me."

Several servants nodded in ascent as Archie held out his hands and accepted the hessian parcel with a beaming smile. The contents would satisfy him for many a day and the cloth would be a precious memento of this day.

Guillem ruffled the boy's hair and turned to the keep's entrance, hunger was calling his name and the tables were splendid in their contents. When he returned to the great hall, his majesty was seated on his throne and several other guests had appeared.

"Good morrow, Guillem, I trust you slept well."

"Very well indeed, sire, thank you. I also managed an early morning jaunt and was excellently guided by the young Archie."

"You are certainly an early riser, Guillem… Archie, you say, which lad would that be?"

"He is the stable boy in charge of my horse, sire, and the very knowledgeable young chap who escorted me earlier."

"I am pleased you are being so well attended. Now enjoy the fare laid before you."

Returning to his seat of the night before Guillem took pleasure in the fine food available. His hunger satisfied, he requested his sovereign's permission to leave and went in search of the mysterious Stephen.

Stephen was refreshing straw in the bedchamber and engrossed in his task, did not immediately sense he was no longer alone. Guillem's voice had him startled.

"Ah, Stephen, there you are."

"Sire, can I be of service?"

"Yes, I have need of your services, when will you complete your morning duties?"

"These quarters are the last requiring my attention, sire. His majesty instructed me to be at your command during your visit. How may I help?"

"I understand that many have pondered your movements, Stephen, I wish to observe you."

Stephen clenched his fists on the broom handle. He would have to be careful. Guillem Ruet was known for his inquiring mind and purposeful examination of all things unusual.

"My movements, sire?"

"Yes, your somewhat unusual pace for want of a better description."

"I walk as others do, sire, although I may have a lighter tread than is usual."

"Maybe so, but I am curious to see you walk at closer quarters."

Mindful of his movements, Stephen made every effort to plant his feet solidly upon the floor as Guillem instructed him to walk back and forth along the corridor. His body tensed at every turn as he saw Guillem's gaze intent upon his feet. It took a great deal of effort to step upon the cold stone. After numerous treks along the corridor, Guillem sighed.

"Well, Stephen, I am at a loss, your tread may be lighter than expected of a man but you certainly do not glide as I imagined when I first saw you. Thank you for your patience at this man's folly."

"At your service, sire. Shall you require anything further?"

"No, thank you. I will take a walk and enjoy the gardens."

Stephen waited until Guillem had turned the far corner before letting out a long held breath. His whole body hurt from the effort of walking as a man. The evening could not come soon enough. Relieved of tiresome duties for the moment he made use of a hidden passageway to the far side of the gardens. His hunger needed sating.

The trimmed hedges and deep red roses were perfectly tended and Guillem sat on a low stone wall to inhale the aroma of foliage and the flower's perfume in the warming sun.

"Guillem?"

"Your majesty, may I be of service?"

"You have found my favorite place for contemplation, Guillem."

"If I have entered forbidden grounds, I shall leave immediately, my queen."

"My gardens are certainly not forbidden, sire; I am pleased to see you are enjoying them."

"It is a very pleasing and well tended garden, your majesty. Is it of your design?"

"Partly; I chose the colour of roses but the hedges have been here for generations. Alas the old rose bushes had woody stems and failed to produce any blooms. I replaced them with vibrant colours to cheer the heart."

"It truly is beautiful, very much like its creator."

"Sire, you will have me blush. Walk with me a while."

The queen settled her hand upon Guillem's arm and they walked slowly throughout the rose garden, followed closely by the queen's attendants. Questions and answers as to the names of certain blooms passed back and forth between them.

"The day's heat is quite overpowering, I shall retire. Thank you, Guillem for a pleasant interlude."

"The pleasure was all mine, as always, I am at your service, majesty."

As the queen disappeared into the castle's interior, Guillem glimpsed Stephen walking swiftly down another path.

Careful to keep at a safe distance behind the mysterious servant, Guillem followed. Observing Stephen's path, he kept close to the shadows of the towering hedges to the edge of the ornamental gardens.

The mysterious servant entered a small copse and disappeared into dappled shade. The trail was partly overgrown; Guillem would have to tread carefully so as not to break any twigs and alert Stephen to his presence. He observed Stephen floating, several inches above the ground, confirming Guillem's suspicions that the young servant had indeed 'acted' out his walking in the castle corridor. Deeper into the copse, a thin veil of cyan mist hung like a curtain. It shimmered as Stephen passed through it and was no more. *What magic is this?* Guillem hesitated. To follow alone would be folly, no-one knew of his whereabouts. He would inform the king of his findings and direct the soldiers to this place. As he had surmised there was more to Silent Stephen than met the eye. There was magic here although yet unknown as to whether it be of evil intent or not.

Chapter Three

Guillem retraced his steps to the rose garden. The hour was later than he expected. *Had the veil changed time?* Upon entering the great hall, all heads turned toward him, expectantly.

"Guillem, I have sent scouts to all corners of my grounds in search of you. Where were you hiding?"

"Your majesty, forgive me. I was in yonder copse. I have a matter of some urgency I must relay."

"Matters can be relayed later, Guillem, my guests and I are anxious to hear the rest of your wonderful tale."

"With all due respect, sire, I feel the tale must wait."

"Wait? I think not, Guillem, we have waited patiently for your appearance. The tale first, then we shall speak."

Not wanting to displease his sovereign, Guillem took his place beside the king's table and began.

"My dialogue of last night had left the lady Lysse watching her lord ride out on his quest to the Dark Mountains and this is where I shall begin."

With a last glance, Lysse re-entered the great hall with her servant, Megan, in tow. Her vigil started from that moment. Unbeknownst to her, the castle guards would have their own vigil protecting her with their lives.

Later, Lysse sat at her chamber window relishing the warmth of the late autumn sun. Her fingers rotated the glass beads at her wrist, turning them again and again. How many days would she have to wait? As the sun set, she admonished herself and resolved to keep busy – time would pass quicker.

She called Megan's name. The servant appeared from the far corner of the chamber, where she had been laying down fresh straw upon the stone tiles.

"Yes my lady."

"Megan, I need to keep myself occupied so I plan to change the drapes in my chamber. We will travel to Datchet on the morrow."

Megan had to think quickly. Lord Elros gave orders Lady Lysse should not leave the castle.

"My lady, I am willing to fetch supplies to save you travelling in the cold."

"Nonsense, Megan, it is a cool autumn day not midst of winter. I have a particular vision for the chamber and need to see the fabrics for myself. We shall ride after breakfast."

Megan nodded her agreement and left the chamber. She must find the captain of the guard and warn him of Lady Lysse's plan. She entered the guard-house to the sound of whet stones upon swords and the smell of leather. A few guards looked appreciatively in her direction as she approached them.

"I have need of the captain, is he here?"

"To the rear and to your right – the captain is inspecting new recruits, Megan."

"Maybe we can entertain you while you wait?"

Megan did not reply but walked determinedly past the many burly men – all busy with some task or another until her appearance. With many eyes watching her she followed the directions she had been given to find the captain talking to three young men. His voice was stern and mirrored in his deep frown.

"To serve Lord Elros is no easy matter. You are expected to lay down your life for your master, willingly. If you have any reservations, leave now."

Two of the young men pulled back their shoulders and said in unison.

"Our Lord and land is worth dying for, Captain."

The other young man stayed silent and bowed his head.

"What say you, Claude?"

"Captain, my father sent me to honor our lord as best I could but I feel I will fail you as a guard. My frame is slight and these men tower above me."

Captain Sylus moved forward and easily picked Claude up. Laughter rang out amongst the other guards.

"Quiet now. This lad may be slight but he obviously has a strong sense of honor to do his father's biding."

The guards turned back to their tasks once more but slyly watched the captain.

"You show courage, Claude, which is an admirable trait but as to your frame, you are right – the weight of a sword would certainly be too great. However, I commend you for attending and I am willing to give you another position within the guard quarters, if you are agreeable."

"Captain, I would be privileged to play a part, however small, in protecting our kingdom."

"Well then, it is settled. You will be my personal attendant from this day forth. The hours will be long and I expect you to do as I ask."

"Thank you, Sir, I will."

The captain gave the lad a pat on the back and set him to work waxing his saddle. It was at this point he noticed Megan standing quietly at the rear of the room.

"Captain Sylus, may I speak with you? It is an urgent matter concerning our lady."

"Well, of course, Megan, I have a few moments before my other inspections begin."

"Lady Lysse is determined to travel to Datchet to purchase supplies. Although I offered to go in her place she refused."

"This is a serious problem, Megan. Lord Elros gave strict instructions she was not to leave the castle. However, to protect her, he also said she was not to be informed of his decision."

"What excuse can we give, Captain?"

"If our Lady Lysse has made up her mind to go, we must conjure up a plausible ruse so that an armed guard would need to accompany her."

"The witch Malgraf and the beast are cause enough surely, Captain Sylus."

"You are right, Megan. She knows of the threat. We will embellish the dangers and tell her there are rumors of Malgraf followers nearing the borders and for her safety we must be extra diligent."

Comforted that her mistress would be safely guarded, Megan returned to her lady's chamber to prepare the bed with a pan of hot coals and lay out her lady's night attire

Early the next morning Megan quickly made her way to the kitchens to inform the cook Lady Lysse would partake of breakfast. Her message delivered she returned to the Lady Lysse's chamber. At the door she heard soft laughter and her lady instructing her other ladies in waiting on the attire she wished to wear. She would return a little later when her lady was properly dressed. Inside the chamber Lysse inspected the offered gowns.

"The burgundy, I think, Ella, and my forest green cape. The air certainly has a chill to it."

"Yes, my lady."

"Shall I gather gloves and a hat as well, my lady?"

"I think that would be wise, Ella."

Lysse turned side to side in front of the mirror. Once satisfied with her appearance she called for Megan to enter.

"Megan, have my bay mare, Saffron, prepared. She is spirited and delights in the cool air."

"As you wish, my lady, I will attend to the matter personally."

A little later, Lysse walked into the courtyard to be faced with a line of mounted guards and Megan holding her mare's reins.

"What is this, Megan? I am riding out to Datchet not battle."

"My lady, due to the potential danger from the witch and the beast, Captain Sylus has ordered a company to ride with us."

"Is that really necessary?"

"Yes, my lady. I will travel with an easier mind knowing we have these men with us. Rumors of Malfian followers have come to the captain's ears."

"Very well, if Captain Sylus thinks it best."

Once her mistress was upon her saddle, Megan straddled her mount and the party rode out under the battlements. The men were ever watchful on the way to the small town but, fortunately, the journey was uneventful and they reached Datchet in good time. Several guards remained outside the merchant's premises with the horses and a couple followed Lysse and Megan into the shop.

A few ladies in his audience exchanged knowing looks encouraging Guillem to embellish details of the store.

Picture if you will, my lords and ladies, a shop's interior with shelves stacked neatly with many luxurious fabrics, while others drape over the walls giving the full effect of their patterning. Fabrics acquired from far lands and sewn by only the finest seamstress' create a rainbow of colours and numerous textures to please the eye. The Lady Lysse looked upon the array with wonderment and pleasure, for she was confident she would find there the fabrics she had in her mind's eye. She was approached by a small balding man with a hunched back. The fabric merchant greeted Lysse with a deep bow and guided her further into his store.

"It is an honor to have you visit my humble store, my lady. How may I be of service?"

"I would like to see all your gold coloured fabrics; I plan to furnish my

lord's chambers while he is travelling."

"It will be my pleasure. I have silks and satins and several heavier velvets that may appeal. If you will excuse me for just a moment I will organize my staff to collect the bolts."

With another deep bow, the man disappeared into the rear of the store, giving orders as he walked. While the owner was absent, Lysse strolled along the many rows of shelves delighting in the textures and colours of bolt after bolt of fabric. As she turned a corner, she gasped in delight at a quilt hanging on the wall. She knew its golden tones and exquisite stitching were a work of art. The piece would be perfect above her marriage bed. With Megan in attendance Lysse surveyed the many yards of quality cloth.

Meanwhile, the owner grabbed a scaly creature from its cage, hidden in the farthest corner of the store. With a few deft strokes he put a note into a small pouch and tied it around the creature's neck. He then pushed the small animal through a hole in the wall. He could hear the echo of its claws scurrying away, down a small tunnel. With the deed done he smiled, confident he would be rewarded for his service.

Laden with luxurious fabrics, he rejoined Lady Lysse and began laying them out for her inspection on a long thin table. The longer he could delay her, the better.

Guillem delighted to gasps from the surrounding tables. The response was why he relished telling tales—to capture an audience and have them completely entranced by his words. Their reactions exhilarated him. His throat was dry. He needed to quench his thirst. As he sipped the ale he noticed all eyes were upon him, anxiously awaiting the next part of the story.

"Shall I continue my majesty? Or is the hour too late?"

"No matter the hour, Guillem, we must know the fate of Elros and Lysse."

"Of course, your highness, as you command."

Stephen chose this moment to surreptitiously slip away. He had an appointment, an important one. One he would not miss even with the threat of punishment for abandoning his post. Making his way along the deepest corridors of the castle, he found the secret opening and pushed the cornerstone. The sound of grating filled the long corridor and Stephen looked back and forth to ensure his exit was not witnessed.

In the great hall, Guillem was as unaware of Stephen's absence as were the other guests. He relayed his tale to a transfixed audience who imagined the merchant's store and wondered at the creature's purpose as Guillem spoke.

Released from the confines of its small cage, the creature hurried along the narrow passage, hunger propelling it to its destination. Cold air blew as light began to invade the darkness.

"Come, my pretty, what do you have for me?"

Gnarled hands grabbed the animal and relieved it of its pouch before dropping it into another small cage. The witch opened the pouch and read quickly.

"You have brought me excellent news, my pet. Have your reward."

The creature's eyes twinkled in the candlelight as a couple of mice dropped in front of it. Crunching sounds immediately followed as tiny skulls were crushed. Malgraf leaned down to watch the feisty creature.

"A disguise is in order to ensure Lady Lysse and her soldiers are off their guard. What shall I use? Ah, yes a shape-shifting spell will suffice. Who can resist a beautiful maiden, one I will inhabit?"

Malgraf opened several jars and collected samples from each and then mixed them together as she chanted.

"Sap of yew and pollen of foxglove
Into another change this form
Leaf of burdock and stem of poppy
Transfix the beholder as I conform."

As the witch caught sight of her familiar's new form, her lips curled in satisfaction. Placing a hand on its forehead she could see through its eyes and control its movements. With a throw of its dark cloak it vanished, intent on arriving at the merchant's store.

Several ladies gasped at Guillem's words and were comforted by their companions. Guillem took a welcomed sip of ale.

In the far corner of the King's grounds, Stephen changed from the human form he detested beyond a cyan veil obscured in a copse. Released from the restrictive form, he was free to stretch his talons and many horned shape. His thick cerulean blue hide and glinting eyes of a turquoise shade unseen in nature would assault many an eye. The sound emitted from this creature was a deep rumbling growl as it searched the land laid out before it. *Where is she - the one that birthed him and will ensure his reign?*

Fingers of frost spread across the ground and he looked up in delight.

"Mother, you have come."

"Spawn of mine; I cannot resist your call."

"The troubadour is taking too long to relay the tale; I feel my bonds breaking through that hideous form."

"I will renew the spell, dear one; you must wait a short time longer. Our time is near although your patience will be stretched; know that he will say those liberating words soon."

"He is suspicious of me—had me walking back and forth like an animal."

"What…impertinent dog—I have just the right hex for him. He will slither under other's feet for all time. Best you stay away from his curious eyes."

"The imposter has me serving him."

"Then you must take extra care to fawn subservience - we are too close to our goal to alert them now."

Chapter Four

Playing his audience as the fine troubadour he was, Guillem changed the story's location to have them hear of Lord Elros' adventure far away from his ladylove in the mountains.

While his lady considered fabrics, Lord Elros and his troop made good time across the plain to the forest edge. As the light faded under a crescent moon, he commanded they set up camp. With their horse's fed and tethered and a hot stew filling their bellies, the men talked around the campfire. Elros walked to the edge of the tree line, carrying a lantern. With a glance about him to ensure he was alone he pulled an aged parchment from his tunic and studied it by the dim light. Eleanor had told him she was certain the map showed a route to the witch's lair. It revealed many traps along the path but with Eleanor's instructions, Elros was certain they would reach their destination. He would have to be precise in his directions to his men to ensure they followed the trail in line with the seer's commands. The sorceress had charmed parts of the forest flora and fauna and many travelers had succumbed to the enchantments with the loss of their life. Elros studied the twisting trails and made mental notes of the many hazards marked with black spots.

As questioning glances were traded in the great hall, Stephen huddled close to his mother comforted by her coldness.

"Your concealing spell has kept my true identity disguised but, at times, I sense the intensity of my eyes break through."

"Keep your head low and pretend to ingratiate yourself. Our time is almost upon us. Temper your anxiousness, my son."

"Yes, mother—magnificence is ours in a few short hours—a century of waiting over."

Blue threads emitted from the witch's fingers and encased the beast – it twisted and reformed into the human form it so despised, whimpering as it was enclosed in the restrictive shape.

"You are truly hideous..."

The witch cackled as her spawn screeched, filling the air around them. Crawling, slithering creatures fled in every direction as the noise sent waves of malevolence outward. The thing called Stephen hobbled back through the veil. Panic gripped the beast as it noticed the twilight. Too long spent within his mother's lands—time slowed when contained therein. He would have to travel swiftly to the castle. Glancing back and forth to ensure he was unobserved, Stephen floated several inches above the ground through the copse and gardens to the castle walls. Another sly peek confirmed he was alone. He pushed a protruding flint inward. A grinding of stone upon stone echoed along a hidden passage. Free to fly within its confines, Stephen travelled swiftly to a concealed panel in the servant's quarters.

After making a few adjustments to his tunic and breeches, he made his way to the great hall where he found the troubadour regaling the tale in front of an engaged audience. Stephen stood in the shadows momentarily then, aware of eyes upon him, he went about his tasks.

Guillem his senses heightened by his suspicions, noticed Stephen's arrival on the far side of the hall, shielded by the shadow of a large pillar as was his disposition. The servant avoided Guillem's eyes as he poured ale for several guests. What had happened through that veil? Guillem was determined to investigate further once his story was at an end. Clearing his throat, he bowed his head, smiled at the assembled crowd and resumed taking them on Lord Elros' path.

Once Elros was satisfied he knew the route, he unrolled his bedroll, placed his sword beside him and slept, safe in the knowledge that the lookouts were alert in their watches throughout the night.

Daybreak saw the troop already awake and hungrily consuming breakfast. Elros joined them in friendly banter until the sun rose sufficiently for him to stand before them.

"Men, we are embarking on a quest to conquer the witch, Malgraf. It will not be without danger and I commend you for volunteering. I am confident we shall succeed."

A cheer rose from his men that echoed through the trees in the early morning mist.

"Saddle up men! We must set forth immediately. Our trek will be arduous

and we must keep our wits about us. Be sure to follow my path exactly. To deviate could mean your demise."

A murmur spread throughout the camp but every man turned to ready himself and his mount. Horses neighed as their girths were tightened, the fire extinguished and the troop filed into the forest. Malgraf would be destroyed this day.

The mist parted as the column advanced revealing an ancient forest of twisted oak trees. The forest floor seemingly writhed with large exposed roots. Each soldier took care to follow the fresh tracks ahead of him as the procession snaked its way deeper and deeper into strange silence. Without the usual bird song and tell tale darting movements of animals, the canopy was eerie. The horses became skittish but, with gentle encouragement, continued to walk forward. A whispered command weaved its way from front to back of the rank.

"Clearing ahead - dismount and disperse around the border."

Breaking left and right in sequence, the riders spanned one side of a large clearing and awaited further commands. The foliage underfoot had a bluish hue to it and the broken sunlight glittered on cyan veined rocks scattered across the whole expanse. On the other side was a larger outcrop of identical rock towering above the meadow.

"There is no way forward – do we turn back before we begin?"

"Lord Elros must have some plan, surely."

"Why come all this way for naught?"

All eyes turned to Lord Elros as he rode into the clearing and turned his mount to face the assembled men.

"Our way forward may seem blocked but be assured, there is magic here. Behold."

Astonished faces watched as Elros gave his mount a gentle kick and proceeded toward the rock face and then…through it. The crag before them parted much like a curtain, with folds flowing back into place once Lord Elros had disappeared from view. The second in command followed at speed concerned as to his master's whereabouts and potential ambush. Equally anxious, the rest of the party followed piercing through the rock face veil to be astonished at the scene before them. An indigo world bathed in a soft radiance similar to moonlight stretched out as far as the eye could see. Midway to the horizon stood a multi-spired azure coloured castle, pointed protrusions covering every wall and tower. In the half light it resembled a dragon's scaly skin. Three moons hung in the navy sky, each with a ring of silver orbiting it.

When Captain Whitlow broke through the veil he breathed a sigh of relief at the sight of Lord Elros and rode to his side.

"This is magic on such a scale that it is difficult for the mind to comprehend, Sire."

"Eleanor spoke of a fantastical land created by Malgraf - she warned me it is filled with beasts and demons disguised as innocents. We must proceed with the utmost care."

"Then it is only fitting that I take the lead, sire, and you have guards posted around you."

"I appreciate your strategy, captain, but I must lead as I have knowledge of the path we are to follow."

"Is it not a task I may take in your place, sire?"

"You have shown me on many occasions that you are competent and willing to take my part, but on this particular quest it is I who will lead."

"As you command, my lord Elros."

The captain nodded in assent and then held up his hand to still the emerging troops as they appeared behind them. Once all were through and assembled, he pronounced.

"Men, the road before us will be filled with obstacles, some of which will be disguised as innocents, keep to the path our lord instructs and do not be deceived by anyone or anything."

"We heed and obey, Captain."

With Lord Elros leading, his captain close to his side, the ranks assembled in single file behind them.

"What of the lady, Guillem?"

"Let us hear of the fight instead."

Guillem held up one hand to still the questioning audience.

"There is much to detail and your impatience is expected but please let me speak as the tale dictates. To tell a part out of sequence will detract from your enjoyment."

"Well said, Guillem, I agree. We must let our distinguished troubadour relay the story as he sees fit."

"Thank you, majesty. With your kind permission I shall continue with Lady Lysse's visit.

The lady was, in fact, still busy choosing cloth and her servant, Megan, was increasingly anxious to have her return to the safety of the castle. The merchant, however, was fawning at the lady's pleasure.

"May I show you some other cloth, my lady?"

"I think the wall hanging and fabrics I have already chosen will suffice. Thank you."

"There is always room for more, surely. I have extra stock in the far store room I could bring for your inspection."

"No, that will be all. Megan take these rolls and the tapestry to the pack animals."

The merchant's hands tightened into fists. He had to delay the lady just a few more moments.

"A warming drink before you go, my lady, to fend off the chill, perhaps?"

"That is a kind offer, but I am impatient to return home. I shall begin my decorating early on the morrow."

Unable to restrain a woman of noble birth, the merchant could only stand and watch her walk out of his store. Fear clasped his heart – what punishment would the sorceress bestow on him for his failure? As the hoof beats faded into the distance he awaited his fate.

Chilled air heralded her arrival; frost caressed the fabrics, walls, and floor. She appeared before the merchant as an indigo vision gradually becoming more tangible.

"She is gone?"

"Mistress, I delayed and delayed..."

"Mere excuses! It was the perfect opportunity. Call yourself a Malfian disciple? You have failed me."

"I will find a way to..."

The words were abruptly cut as the merchant disintegrated into a small pile of blue ash. Malgraf's familiar's long cloak enfolded her and she vanished. She never gave second chances to insignificant beings especially those who failed her.

Dust swirled behind the troop's horses as they flanked Lady Lysse on the journey back to the castle, unaware of a dark cloud high above them. Malgraf could bide her time for a while longer but she sensed a change – a change that excited her. Soon the ancient prophecy would be fulfilled. Her spawn of Horthen would reign these outer lands, consuming them, bending all who languished there to the ways of Malgraf magic.

Again Guillem's sudden halt in the proceedings had the lords and ladies gasping and whispering to each other.

"Forgive me, your majesties, lords and ladies, but I have supped too much ale and have to take my leave for a moment."

Laughter rang out around the hall and several other attendees took advantage of the respite. Once all were again assembled, Guillem returned to his tale watched intently by all, including Silent Stephen, whose blue eyes flared with an inner light. The enchantment spell would be spoken soon and he would be released from his earthly trappings. His muscles twitched in anticipation as the troubadour once again entered the great hall and took his place. As Guillem began speaking again Stephen shuddered, soon he would feast on flesh. The troubadour's voice filled the hall with only the occasional whisper or thud of a tankard intruding an attentive silence.

"We had Elros and his troop within the magical realm of the witch, Malgraf, and we shall follow their journey."

All senses were heightened amongst Lord Elros' troops as they travelled toward the multi-towered castle. Fleeting glimpses of movement had each man turn this way and that in attempts to fully comprehend what their eyes perceived as pointed heads, slithering tails and bright blue eyes piercing through the darkness. A shout broke the silence from the rear flank. As one, the column turned, swords ready to fight. Two soldiers hung in midair, their necks obviously broken but jangling as if still alive held by great dark claws. An enormous creature towered above the soldiers growling and baring large fangs.

"Make ready, men. Today we slay a creature of Malgraf's creation."

Frantic slicing, stabbing and cutting commenced as the troop surrounded the beast. It fought fiercely, throwing men and horses alike as if they were mere puppets. Claws split men and horses in two as if they were cloth. Screams and snorts accompanied by deep growling filled the air. Steel clashed against scale, fang and claw against shield. Although many blades found their target, the beast would not succumb. Dark blood oozed from numerous wounds yet the beast's strength and power were evident.

"Captain, charge to the right as I charge to the left. The beast will die this day!"

"My lord, our blades do not pierce deeply enough. Its heart must be our target."

"Use the lances, command the men to focus on its breast."

With renewed effort, the two flanks charged the beast head on. The sharp tipped lances aimed at its mid chest and the other ends secured on the frozen ground. As the animal moved forward, the tips found entry under scale and tissue. At last the beast met its demise eventually overcome by the sheer number of assailants. With its last breath exhaled, some of the troops collapsed to the ground in exhaustion while others cut scales from the creatures hide as souvenirs. Elros watched the last glint of turquoise extinguish from its eyes.

Guillem stopped short… *turquoise eyes, where had he seen them?* He turned toward the rear of the hall searching for Stephen. *Could he be a familiar?*

"Come now, Guillem, do not leave us in suspense, what of Elros and his men?"

"Your majesty, if you will pardon me, I respectfully request an audience with you, alone."

"An audience? But you have one sat afore you, my man. What can be so important as to leave us all in trepidation?"

"I fear this tale has hidden depths and meaning, my lord. To continue may be our undoing."

"Ah, I see part of the act… very good, my troubadour. Now, continue the hour grows late."

"But…"

"Must I command you, man?"

"No, my lord."

Guillem's heart beat fiercely as he resumed anxiousness apparent as his voice shook with emotion. *What would his words unleash?* With consternation, he continued with a lick of his lips, dry from talking for so long.

Stephen stood behind Guillem his head lowered. He needed to probe this man's mind—the tale recited was not only a secret but also sacred to Stephen and the other followers.

Chapter Five

Expectant and attentive faces before him, Guillem continued.

With the creature dead, Lord Elros walked along the trail, inspecting the wounded and able bodied, assessing the result of the encounter. To fail now would be catastrophic to his kingdom. He needed as many able men as possible to storm the castle and slay the evil sorceress, Malgraf.

"Men, we have come far into this strange world. I ask that the ones among you who are able to accompany me further do so. Our onward trek is bound to be even more treacherous. The witch will likely have beasts guarding her inner domain."

Eyes fixed on their lord, the soldiers nodded as one, in agreement.

"You honor me with your sense of duty, men. We shall conquer the evil that is Malgraf."

With a few medics left behind to tend to the wounded, Elros led his troops closer to the castle. Resolve pumping their blood for the fight to come.

Within yards of the castle keep, a frozen mist gathered around the column obscuring the drawbridge.

"Hold fast men, it is the witch's doing. Follow the sound of my commands and beware surprise attacks from every direction."

Loud buzzing filled the ghostly white air and the troops were subjected to hundreds of stinging bugs bombarding them. Swords swatted at the beasts resulting in drips and splats of blue ooze covering man, horse and ground, alike.

"Stay focused and move forward. Do not delay."

With their captain's words ringing in their ears, the soldiers surged forward as one. Hooves sounded on wooden planks as confirmation they were indeed entering the castle. The captain's voice echoed against the castle walls.

"Take heed - have your wits about you, men. The sorceress is capable of powerful magic and has been known to bewitch many an unsuspecting victim. Do not believe your eyes or ears unless it is mine or our lord's voice or face before you. Hold true to your basic senses."

From her vantage point on the battlements, Malgraf smiled a crooked smile. Such simple minds were no match for her magic. Mere men were easily fooled. She watched as the column filed into her inner courtyard. She would delight in bewitching them.

Once inside the castle walls, Elros signaled his men to form a circle facing outward so their backs were to each other. Massive doors adorned with glittering jewels stood before Elros, flanked by dark twisting stonework, much like vines. He dismounted, as did his captain, and with a hand signal, the rest of the horsemen followed suit.

"Venture forth, with caution, in groups of three – on my command, and my command alone, enter the corridors in search of the witch. She can only be slain with the cutting off of her head. No other wound will suffice."

As instructed, the men split into trios and, on the order, advanced into passages, branching out from the courtyard.

Malgraf raised a hand and sprinkled teal dust on several men standing closest to the battlement below her. Unaware they were bewitched, the trio entered a corridor to their right. Stonework covered in carved vines, strange clawed creatures and a dark seeping substance kept the men vigilant. A blue glow shone ahead, drawing them toward it. An opened door revealed a table laden with a sumptuous feast. The aroma was too tantalizing to ignore. The possession of their minds was complete. Each man plunged as if starved and began devouring the succulent meats. Mouths dripping with meat juices, each man's hunger became all consuming. Forgotten was their quest or any danger that may befall them. Mouthful after mouthful eaten; still the hunger could not be sated. The table cleared every plate emptied and their contents devoured, the men searched for more, crazed with hunger until they fell upon each other for sustenance. Flesh was ripped, torn, bitten and consumed in a frenzied mania. Malgraf's satisfied laughter rang out in the chamber.

She would have more fun this day. Gliding within a cyan mist, Malgraf found her next victims creeping along another corridor. What delight could she play upon these men? A twist of her fingers had the stone vines detach from the walls and slither up the men's legs and bodies. Their cries where quickly silenced as the coils squeezed the air from the men's lungs and crushed bone and tissue.

Alerted by the sudden shouts, Elros bade his group to stand fast. They stood within a great hall decorated with floating sapphire orbs while blue flames flickered within the enormous hearth and an elaborate throne sat at the far end.

"This is surely Malgraf's seat; she will trick and bewitch us all if we do not take care. The cries you hear could be real but equally not."

Elros took the parchment out of his tunic and began reciting the words Eleanor had discovered.

Guillem stammered as he glimpsed intense turquoise eyes flaring from the shadows. *Was this what the strange servant was waiting for? What would the words unleash?* He had to delay this part of the story until he spoke to the king.

"Your majesty, lords and ladies, my tale will further delight you tomorrow evening. The fate of Lord Elros and his lovely lady will be played out to its conclusion."

Guillem's audience let out a sigh in unison with some protests that he managed to quell. As the hall emptied of guests, Guillem approached his king and bowed deeply.

"Your majesty, please forgive me, but I must talk with you. It is a matter of the greatest importance."

"Really, at this late hour, Guillem? Surely it can wait 'till morning."

"I fear to delay will have dire consequences."

Noticing the sincerity in Guillem's voice, the king kissed his lady's hand and bade her goodnight. Once the queen had left the room, Guillem held up his hand and put a finger to his lips. The king frowned but kept silent. Motioning to the guard, Guillem had them search every part of the great hall paying close attention to the stone pillars. Stephen was nowhere to be found, however Guillem was nervous that magical forces may be present.

"May we retire to the throne room, majesty?"

At the king's questioning glance, Guillem lowered his voice to a whisper.

"Treachery is afoot, sire and best we talk in secure surroundings."

With guards posted outside the doors and at strategic points around the magnificent throne chamber, Guillem spoke.

"Your majesty, I have reason to believe the tale I am relaying is in fact part of an elaborate plot to over throw your crown and plague these lands with evil."

"How can the telling of a tale have such an effect, Guillem?"

"The last part of the story includes an incantation. It is my belief those words will release an evil force, in fact, the very same evil I recite, Malgraf."

"Your stories are certainly powerful and compelling, Guillem, but releasing malicious powers? I think not. Are you ailing or maybe consumed bad meat?"

"Sire, I followed Stephen through the gardens to a copse on the far side of your castle walls. He entered a veil of mist and disappeared but not before I witnessed his ability to float above the ground. It is my suspicion that he is a familiar of the witch, Malgraf. I feared I would not return so did not proceed to follow him as I would have wished."

"You will show me this copse and veil at first light. If there are secret forces therein I will destroy them."

"Firstly, you must apprehend Stephen and imprison him. He is a link we best break."

"Guards search the castle and grounds! Stephen is to be brought before me by daybreak."

In the deep dark recesses of the apex of the roof, Stephen floated above the conspirators. Their feeble attempts to conquer the power waiting to be released were laughable. Crawling upside down, he quietly opened a concealed trapdoor onto the uppermost battlements. He must retrieve the orb before returning to his mother.

The castle echoed with soldier's feet stomping through every corridor, chamber and hall. Shouted commands and directives filled the night but Stephen could not be found. It was easy to evade capture with his knowledge of the hidden passageways and the ability to walk upon the ceilings. He delighted in the spectacle of so many men hurrying about the castle in their fruitless search.

At daybreak, as the king commanded a regiment of troops gathered in the courtyard. Their captain sat upon a fine white stallion facing his men and addressed them.

"Men, we head out today in search of an enemy unlike any we have fought before. We now know that the evil suspected by Guillem is that of Malgraf, a fearful and malicious opponent. Be sure in your hearts that the battle ahead of us will be hard won. It has been my privilege to serve with you. We go into battle with honor and pride to serve our sovereign."

A great cheer rose from the ranks accompanied by fists beating against shields. A war cry if ever there was one. The captain saluted his men and turned his mount toward the drawbridge. In slow procession, the rank filed behind him and Guillem, who was riding beside their leader.

Guillem could feel the excitement of the troops emanate from them; their eagerness to do battle was evident. With a raised hand the captain commanded to move forward at a canter resulting in a plume of dust rising from the horses' hooves. The sky blushed pink as the column made its way to the copse. At Guillem's acknowledgment, the captain halted his troops before the trees and addressed Guillem.

"Best you stay here, Guillem. I will leave a couple of men with you. Corde, Steele, at the first signs of trouble get back to the castle and return with all the regiments. If this goes wrong, it's going to go very wrong; I can feel it in my bones."

"Sir, yes sir."

The two men thumped their fists against their chests in salute. Guillem watched as the mounted soldiers wound their way into the copse. He wished them well in their endeavor but still, his skin prickled, fearful that their force would be easily matched and ultimately overcome.

The orb blazed in Stephen's hand the nearer he got to the veil. Once beyond it, he would discard the cumbersome human shape for the last time. He would not return to the castle as a spy ever again, but as the rightful ruler, side by side with his mother. Hoof beats sounded far behind him alerting him the search had been extended from the castle and its gardens. Their feeble attempts to pursue him made him smile; they had no idea of the power soon to be brought down upon this land. It would vanquish all without exception. The veil parted as he glided through, his disguise dropping away to reveal the scaly skin and thorn like protrusions along his back.

The beast fell to all fours and sprinted along a narrow trail towards a dark castle in the distance, his home. His mother would be waiting, an empty throne beside her—his rightful place. The creature moved with ease, enjoying the freedom of its natural shape, howling as it went. At the drawbridge, he rose up onto his hindquarters and bayed to the moons. Once inside, he raced along twisting corridors to his mother who sat with arms out stretched.

"Come, my son. Our time is but hours away."

Arms embraced scaly hide and hot breath whispered across the witch's face. Her violent coupling with the Horthen had left her scarred, but her son was worth all the agony and tearing. She had kept his birth a secret and shortly before her imprisonment, had disguised her son as a human with a simple transformation spell. Then she used a false memory spell for the inhabitants of the court, making Stephen a fixture and beyond suspicion. He was her link to the outer world and a valuable informer.

Once Malgraf was released, she knew, together, she and her son would reign supreme for all time. The disgusting verdant greens and horrid floral colours would be swept away to be replaced with cyan, turquoise, teal and blue hues relieving the abomination that so assaulted their eyes. Her son then looked up with his turquoise eyes, satisfaction within their depths.

"The story teller is close to the enchantment part of the tale, Mother, but I am pursued and shall not be able to return to capture the queen."

"It is a small glitch that can be overcome. I shall mask my true being as one of her ladies in waiting. The wench ventures to the rose garden alone—often."

"May I capture her?"

"Ensure you bring back enough blood so I may make the transformation potion. The rest you may consume, you must be ravenous."

"So little meat was to be had within the castle but I consumed several cattle under the cover of darkness each night."

"You are truly resourceful, my son. No-one tracked you or fretted over the missing animals?"

"The peasants believed a devil was eating their animals and surrounded the village with herbal potions. It was amusing to watch."

"Pathetic beings, all of them, their meat shall satisfy my pets once the portal opens."

"I have the seeking orb with me. Do you wish to see their movements?"

"Place it upon my lap; let us enjoy a little sport."

With the orb laid before her the witch passed her hands over it and an internal mist cleared showing the troops rushing toward the copse. Mother and son watched intently as three men stayed at the edge of the tree line while the rest, forty or more entered the woods.

Once the last man was through the veil Malgraf held the orb and began casting a spell.

"Twisting, turning path,
Snake your way hither and thither.
Plunge into torrents deep and dark.
Minds confuse energy drain."

Within the confines of the orb the two conspirators gleefully observed the troop's gradual annihilation as the path ridden twisted back on its self time and time again, hazard after hazard was overcome at the expense of a few more soldiers at each encounter. As their stamina grew less and less —more and more men fell behind to be taken by creatures of abhorrent features. With no more than ten victims left the young beast could contain himself no longer.

"I am in need of blood; Mother with so few left none will make the castle walls."

"Then go, enjoy. We have time before I am in need of the wench's essence."

Chapter Six

Standing vigil at the edge of the copse, Guillem and his companions grew anxious.

"The captain would surely have returned afore now?"

"Aye, you may be right, best we make our way back to report."

"Should we not attempt a rescue?"

"Ney, captain was adamant we should not follow him. Let us make sure the troubadour returns safe and sound for tonight's feast and report to the king."

Flanked by the soldiers, Guillem dropped his head despairing of the loss of life for surely no-one survived beyond the veil. Urgency overtook the trio and they were swiftly at a full gallop across the fields.

The thundering hooves had peasants scatter before them as they approached the castle. Cobbles and stone walls resonated with their entry drawing guards and servants to the central courtyard with anxious faces and pounding hearts. The three men dismounted and took the steps to the keep two at a time. The king must be informed immediately.

"We have word of Captain Ruden—the king must know."

Two sentries escorted them along the corridors to the throne chamber. Taking several deep breathes to allay their disquiet, the soldiers and Guillem proceeded through the great doors and settled on one knee in front of their king.

"What news?"

"Your majesty, we fear the captain and all other lives have been lost beyond the bewitched veil. We witnessed no sight or sound for these long hours."

"You did not venture forth?"

"Our captain was most insistent we did not follow, but report back to you and garner more troops to storm the witch's lair."

"If her power is so great against forty or so men within that enchantment I cannot, in good heart, send another forty or more. We must lure her onto our own battle ground."

"You are most wise, my lord, I detect a plan."

"A plan I have been formulating in the past several hours, Guillem, but one that will have to remain undisclosed until the time is right."

"Your majesty, if I may be of service, I am at your beck and call."

"Indeed, you will play a pivotal part, my storyteller but for now you must rest, for tonight the details will be decided."

Guillem bowed and made his way up to his quarters. He entered cautiously fearing Stephen may be waiting or some other strange beast intent on harm. The room was empty and his belongings as he had left them. Reassured he was indeed alone he lay down to rest his eyes for a moment. A thudding woke him with a start. *Had he slept so deeply he was unaware of his surroundings or anyone near him?*

"Who is at my door?"

"Archie, sire, I've been sent to wake you."

"Come in my young lad while I wipe away the sleep from my eyes."

"The king requires an audience with you in the throne chamber. There have been many goings on as you slept."

"Such as?"

"Guards placed around the great hall, no excuses accepted for leaving or entering the castle these two hours, and now the drawbridge has been raised."

"Curious indeed, Archie. Well, I am ready; let us proceed to the king's chamber without delay."

Escorted by his young friend, Guillem was guided back to the king's room, its magnificent doors shielded by six sentries. They brandished their spikes. Guillem stood waiting for the command to enter. There was the sound of a heavy latch releasing and a deep rasping heralded the door opening.

"You may enter, Guillem Ruet, the king will see you now."

The servant swept his hand toward the interior and with effort closed the door behind Guillem. The king was standing at a great table with a large parchment covering its surface.

"There you are, Guillem, come we must organize the details of tonight's agenda."

"Tonight, your majesty, are we not laying a trap in which to ensnare the witch and her beast?"

"To ensure success we must disguise our actual intent, Guillem. Malgraf has powerful resources at her command. We must be sly in our dealings with her, catch her off guard."

With great care taken, to every detail, the two men planned the evening's program over the next hour. Guillem mentally ran through the tale being careful not to voice certain parts he felt may be dangerous. One such incantation caught his attention, the words held power he could feel burning into his mind.

"It would be best if I omitted some words, my majesty—we do not know of their influence."

"You are right to be circumspect, Guillem. It is this very reason I consort the wisdom of a soothsayer. A woman of such great age even she cannot remember how many years she has been on this earth."

"Where can we find such a woman, sire?"

"Actually right here, Guillem, I present Elviva and her granddaughter, Juliana."

Guillem had been unaware of the women when he first entered the throne room, hidden as they were by deep shadows at the rear of the room. It wasn't until the king called their names did Guillem become conscious that he and his sovereign were not alone. A wizened old lady shuffled her way towards them aided by a striking looking woman, who took Guillem's breath away. Her beauty stunned him into silence.

"Is this he?"

"This indeed is the troubadour I told you about, Elviva."

"The tale you tell, is it of your own making?"

"I…well it is in some manner…the tale came to me in a dream."

The old woman grasped Guillem's hand, her flesh thin, akin to paper.

"As I suspected she has bewitched you storyteller. The tale you tell is of her design for some dark purpose. Tell me are you near story's end?"

"My narrative will conclude this very evening."

"Are there incantations within?"

"Yes, words I shall not speak as they burn in my mind. I dare not voice them."

"I shall need parchment and quill, majesty."

"Take what you require, Elviva, there is plenty at your disposal here."

The old woman beckoned her granddaughter closer and whispered into her ear. Guillem watched the young woman divide the parchment into six pieces and dip the quill into ink.

"You will recite the first two lines of the incantation to me while Juliana notes them."

"But… will we not incur the wrath of Malgraf?"

"It is only when the words are spoken in their rightful order do they release their power. Follow my instructions precisely and the evil shall be contained."

Guillem relayed the words in the order, Elviva directed while Juliana wrote them on separate pieces of parchment.

"Careful not to let the edges touch or to read the words together, my child."

"As you say, Eldenma."

At the strange endearment, Guillem looked up at Juliana. Their eyes locked and he experienced a yearning never before felt. Such dark eyes… seemingly fathomless.

"No time, story teller for other matters, let us continue."

The old woman's husky voice broke into his trance. *How could this maiden entrance him so—had he not had his fill of willing maidens?*

"The last lines will be spoken separately and noted the same."

Juliana moved the last piece of parchment to the opposite end of the table and then stood at her grandmother's side.

"Your majesty, there is a part of this ritual that requires you play a part."

"Elviva, I am willing to assist if it means destroying the sorceress. What will you have me do?"

"Blood must be spilt…"

"Blood, come now, is this necessary?"

"Quite necessary, sire, for without it the papers will assemble releasing the words then no amount of fighting will conquer the pure evil contained therein."

"We must be guided by Elviva, Guillem; I have every reason to trust her."

"Your majesty, I shall be guided by your example."

Elviva unsheathed a small dagger that caught the firelight on its blade. With a deft movement she pierced her palm and let blood drop onto one part of the transcript. Juliana held out her hand and did not flinch when the blade cut, even though Guillem did. Not wanting to be diminished in the maiden's eyes Guillem held out his palm. The dagger sliced, beads of blood seeped onto another page. Then Elviva faced the king who nodded his ascent. His hand was steady as the soothsayer punctured it with the blade's tip. Each of the six sections were smeared with blood and cast into the fire. As the parchment burnt, flames of intense purple flared, all the while Elviva chanted under her breath.

"I shall fashion new words for you to speak, tale teller, which will reveal those shielded by magic. His majesty has made provision for extra guards within the great hall, I do believe."

"Indeed, Elviva, some disguised as servants and others as courtiers concealing our true number to tackle any opposition."

"More parchment, Juliana."

Guillem watched as Juliana gently placed more parchment before her elderly companion and then dipped the quill into the ink. The insertion of the quill had his thoughts on delights he could enjoy with this enticing maid. The quill tip scratched across the dry paper. Elviva's hand shook making the letters spidery in form.

"Read what I have written, Guillem, but do not voice it. If you are unsure of a word please point it out to me."

Guillem took the offered paper and read the text. The scribble before him took some time to decipher but he did manage to read every line. He nodded his understanding to Elviva.

"My part is done, your highness. If I may take my leave, this work leaves me undone."

"You have been of great service this night, Elviva; I have made arrangements for you to stay within the castle tonight."

"A kindness most welcome, thank you."

Juliana helped her elderly grandmother to her feet and, with a small curtsy escorted her from the room. Guillem could only watch as the beautiful woman left, his thoughts on making her acquaintance distracting him as the king spoke.

"You will have time enough for pleasures, Guillem, but for now our task is not quite finished."

"Forgive me, sire, the maid has me affected."

The king laughed in good humor.

"That my dear fellow, is obvious, your colour high, your breath hurried. After this evening's plot concludes we shall both have time for more pleasurable pursuits?"

"I sincerely hope that will be the case, sire."

With a few more details rehearsed, and satisfaction gained, the two men shared ale in front of the hearth. Their apprehension at the task ahead of them hidden from the other. Execution of the event hung on fine timing.

"The hour is almost upon us, Guillem; I shall retire to my quarters to dress for the evening. With luck our morrow will see us victorious."

"That is my greatest hope as well, your majesty. I shall see you at the feast."

Chapter Seven

Guillem exited the throne chamber and made his way along the main passageway toward his quarters. As he turned a corner he collided with Juliana causing her to drop a basket, its contents spilling in every direction.

"Forgive me, sire."

Her face flushed as she bowed her head.

"Entirely my fault, Juliana; I was a little distracted with the evening's plans. Let me assist you, please."

"There is no need, sire, I can manage."

"But it would please me to, Juliana."

As they gathered herbs, small vials and pebbles from the stone floor their hands touched occasionally, which sent delightful shivers along Guillem's arms.

"If my presence at the feast was not required this evening, I would certainly enjoy time in your company."

"You honor me with such a proposition, sire, I am but a lowly maid."

"I strongly disagree, Juliana. You are far from lowly."

Guillem smiled as a flush rose on Juliana's face. She gave a small curtsy to allow her to hide her embarrassment.

"I will not keep you longer, Juliana, but I would be pleased to spend some time with you once we have succeeded with our evening's venture. Would you consider allowing me?"

"Sire, I am not at liberty to make that decision, but if you command then I shall obey."

"I shall not command you, Juliana, I wish you to make the choice as you would for any man requesting to court you."

"Court…me? Sire, I am…

"Forgive me, Juliana, for being so bold. I will let you ponder my words and let you about your chores."

"Thank you, sire."

Guillem observed Juliana as she hurried away along the corridor. *Why had he confessed his desires so freely?* He had no time to dally on such things just now. Striding back to his quarters he tried to keep his mind on the details of the evening's plan but Juliana's face penetrated his thoughts. Any other maid he would have been quick to satisfy his needs then continued without a backward glance. Juliana was certainly different.

With a concerted effort, Guillem managed to review the new words given to him and he also timed himself reading the last part of the story. As he sat in his chamber his mind waivered into the depths of dark eyes—he had to actually shake his head to disperse the images. Juliana had such a hold on his thoughts—something Guillem was unaccustomed to. Mentally scolding himself he rehearsed his opening speech again. Tonight was not the time to be distracted by a maid—there was a great deal at stake including his own life.

The allotted hour arrived and Guillem dressed with care so he could conceal a large dagger within his clothing. Elviva had been insistent on him carrying it. She had mumbled words and made strange hand movements over the horn handled dagger. A spell she told Guillem that would ensure unnatural beings would perish once they were cut with its blade. Its weight evident against his chest reassured Guillem—tonight would see victory for the king.

The great hall was a cacophony of sound - talking guests, minstrels playing and singing, servants hurrying back and forth with platters and tankards. Guillem took in a deep breath, *tonight would be his greatest performance yet—best be perfect,* his mind echoed.

"Our honored guest does arrive, lords and ladies, if you are as anxious as I you will fill your tankards and attend his words."

Guillem nodded his thanks to the king before taking his place at the small table previously reserved for him.

"Tonight, I wish you to relay your tale from the high table, Guillem. Please make your way up here beside me."

Several puzzled looks were exchanged amongst the assembled audience but none were so brave as to question their king. Guillem stood slightly behind his sovereign's ornate throne and to one side. A hush spread throughout the room as the king nodded his consent for Guillem to begin. Undetected by the lords and ladies were numerous guards in disguise around the room; Guillem noticed a few familiar faces from the guard room. Everyone was unaware of the presence of several beings cloaked by magic who floated in concentric circles above the banquet tables.

With a slight clearing of his throat, Guillem began, stilling his nerves by clinching his fists behind his back.

"Last evening you will remember, I trust, Lord Elros had entered the witch's realm."

There was a general nodding of heads amongst the audience.

"I shall return us to the witch's lair."

With a contingent of men gathered in the great hall alongside him, Elros bade them search for an ebony engraved box with a beast's head upon the lid. Eleanor had advised him that the box contained an incantation that would destroy the witch and her beasts. Malgraf succeeded in stealing it decades earlier from a wizard, who had entombed the witch in a glass sphere a century earlier. He placed the sphere in an alcove but it was accidentally broken by the wizard's apprentice. Once released Malgraf had slaughtered the wizard and all who resided in his realm. Her attempts at destroying the parchment, however, had failed thus leaving her no choice but to encase it in a spell protected container. Although Eleanor knew of the container she could not help Elros with its location.

"Be thorough in your search men, the successful culmination of our venture depends on its discovery."

Every nook and cranny of the room was delved into until a cry came from a darkened corner.

"Sire, is this not what we search for?"

Lord Elros approached the young soldier who held out a black box toward him. Exactly as described, the box was as black as pitch emblazoned by a beast's head with gleaming jade eyes. With a steady hand and relief in his heart, Elros took the proffered object.

"We shall conquer this night..."

Elros' words were cut short as a spiral of teal mist drifted down from the ceiling and took the form of a witch. Swords were brandished as the men surrounded their lord. Elros secreted the box underneath his cloak.

"Do you think mere swords can defeat me? I can slice you all in two with a lift of a finger and feed the scraps to my familiars."

"Malgraf, we have the means to vanquish you, make no mistake. Tonight is your last."

"Brave words coming from a mere mortal – your strength is an illusion – witness my strength."

With a sweep of her hand several soldiers rose upward to be impaled upon spears held by gargoyles, which moments previously had been merely stonework decoration. Now these creatures crawled down the arches and pillars around the room, slicing and piercing flesh as they encroached upon the circle of soldiers. Malgraf's laughter rang out as she delighted in the scene before her. Blood flowed in every direction channeled between the stone slabs and disappeared into the earth in-between them. Another sweep of her hand had the stone vines animated – slithering across the floor. Each vine encircled a leg or arm, then with deliberate unhurried purpose pulled the men asunder filling the great hall with agonized screams and pleas of help.

Hidden by numerous shields from Malgraf's view, Elros struggled to open the box. Its latch was made of a strange cyan coloured metal and, with no obvious key hole, Elros had to think quickly. Placing the object on the floor he whispered his intent to the soldiers nearest him. They moved away slightly keeping their shields high while Elros withdrew his sword, swung it high above his head and cleaved the box in two. Hastily, he retrieved the parchment that rolled from it.

"Take heart men I have our salvation at hand."

Elros held the two halves of the parchment together and began reciting the words written thereon.

Guillem saw his audience take a breath as one—enraptured with the events he relayed. Now was the true test of the plan, these words would reveal the witch's beasts and in reality destroy her—no longer a story, but reality, many would not fully comprehend. In the meeting held earlier, the King's captain advised that panic would ensue within the chamber once the magical beings appeared. He suggested not only the disguised guards within the hall, but also a contingent hidden just outside, enter at a particular word or signal. The king had agreed. As he surveyed the room feeling the tension as everyone waited with bated breath, he noted the king's hands were also clasped tightly upon his lap where a large dagger lay as well as the entrapment orb. A slight nod from his majesty gave Guillem his signal to continue.

Shielded from the dangers surrounding him, Elros recited the words before him.

As he read the incantation orbs crashed to the floor, flames flashed blue and gold in the hearth. The vines ceased their advance; the gargoyles once again became stone wherever they crawled.

"By air and earth, sky and sea, keep harm from us. Power that binds upon this place take flight – your shade will fall, your true shape will reveal. Henceforth forever more banish the enchantment upon this place, giving substance nevermore."

Guillem's last few words were lost in a clamor of sound that broke out around him as creatures were revealed; soldiers stormed in or discarded their disguises to battle the familiars. Lords swept their ladies behind them with one arm while wielding their swords with the other. Terror filled the women's eyes while determination filled their partner's eyes. The creatures' disadvantage at being suddenly revealed was fully utilized. Each one squealed as it was sliced in two or silenced abruptly as it was beheaded. The beasts were quickly overpowered and disposed forthwith. The oozing bodies spasmodically twitched before becoming forever still.

The captain shouted orders to have all the guests escorted out quickly and the heavy oak doors closed. Only a few elderly men left the great hall with the women, the rest stayed pledging allegiance to their sovereign.

"Your majesty, for your own safety, I graciously request you vacate."

"Captain, I understand your reservations in my staying, but this is one battle I have to fight."

Guillem drew his own dagger; his eyes searched the uppermost corners of the chamber. *Was she watching them?* The last part of the incantation rolled over and over in his mind—anxiousness jumbling the words. He admonished himself—recite as Elviva instructed or we all die.

Malgraf's eyes turned jade as her anger increased at the sight of her creature's slaughter. She searched the crowded hall for the king - he would die first and in the chaos that ensued she would slay all others who dared defy her. The incantation held no strength against her own spell of invisibility – they knew not her true strength but they certainly would. Descending in the shadow of a pillar she transformed into the shape of a soldier and walked directly toward the king, making comments of the horrors so as not to raise suspicion.

Her target, King Henry, was deep in conversation with the captain and unaware of her approach.

"Why did the witch not reveal herself, sire?"

"There are more words to be spoken, captain, but we must choose our time to relay them. Too soon and she will escape—too late…well, that is not going to happen."

"Elviva was quite insistent that Guillem look into Malgraf's eyes as he speaks. The power of the spell will penetrate and ensure victory."

"How can he do such a thing…she is nowhere to be seen?"

A cry from behind them had the two men turn quickly to face several soldiers clashing swords with one other. As the blades struck, the single man shimmered as if under water and reformed into the witch.

"You dare defy me—you will all die slowly at my hand."

"Now, Guillem, now is the time."

Guillem looked at the witch and began reciting as the guards surrounding him fought against her.

"Willow branch, acorn seed, foxglove juice, and nightshade bloom, infuse together and smite the evil here tonight. Strength will seep, form will dissolve—no longer be."

Malgraf's scream pierced ears causing some to bleed at its pitch. Tendrils of mist appeared from under her cloak and she shimmered.

"You shall not entomb me again—jade and jet your strength do bestow, repel those against me."

Guillem stuttered as Malgraf focused on him, slicing a man in two with her sword as she drew closer to him. Man after man was repelled as if mere phantoms—their vigor seemingly diminished.

"Do not hesitate, Guillem, read and hold this orb tightly."

At his sovereign's stern command Guillem continued, though his voice shook with trepidation at the witch's advance. His grip on the glass orb grew tighter—the vessel that would imprison her forever—if he could only impart the final words successfully.

"Light of purity shine, disperse shadow and darkness, split asunder that which burdens this land. Caste away darkened power, fragment this evil..."

As Guillem completed the incantation Malgraf rose up a hand in a last attempt to destroy her persecutors. She tossed darts of dark light upwards which then fragmented flying in many directions around the hall. Small spiny creatures burst from stone engravings throwing dust about them then crashing to the floor to bite and claw. They were easily dispensed with sword and dagger. Flames flashed orange and red in the hearth. Malgraf once again felt pain as surely as a blade cuts.

"Avoid the dust, men it is enchanted. Use your shields to prevent it falling onto your skin."

All shields were raised in unison as the assembled troops observed the misty threads above them swirl in ever decreasing circles.

Guillem's eyes grew wide as Malgraf's sword dropped to the stone slabs sending sparks upward. Cyan droplets billowed around and through the witch's body her eyes flashed turquoise as a funnel began to form. Its tip headed straight for the orb which glowed brightly in Guillem's hands.

"Mother…" Stephen's husky pleading voice emerged from a crippled beast huddled beside the hearth. It slowly crawled toward Malgraf's diminishing image as its vapor was drawn into the orb.

"Son…do not part…"

The voice heard was that of Malgraf but its source was unclear—heads turned this way and that in vain attempts to locate its origin. The creature that was once called Stephen reached up to catch the misty threads. Before astonished faces it too vaporized although turquoise in colour. The cyan and turquoise tendrils entwined as they were sucked into the orb's interior. Swirling in ever faster circles within their enclosure until the orb began to vibrate. Guillem gripped it firmly fearful of dropping it and releasing its contents.

"Her power is diminished—we have destroyed the one named Malgraf."

A roaring cheer rang out but before congratulatory pats on the back could begin a flare of white light bathed the great hall. Ready for another attack the assembled fighters turned toward the great oak doors. There stood Elviva and Juliana radiant in white robes and each holding golden staffs. Soldiers parted as the two women made their way to Guillem and the King. The brightness of their attire made eyes squint at its power, a complete contrast to the darkness that just held the room. Juliana gave a deep curtsy while Elviva bowed her head.

"My lord, you have done well. I will take possession of the orb—it will be taken far away where it will be sheathed in an entrapment spell forever."

With great care, Guillem held out the orb toward Elviva, his heart skipped a beat when he saw her hands shaking. *Surely it would fall.* Juliana placed her hands above her grandmother's and took the vibrating orb. Relief washed over Guillem, so much so he felt dizzy with it. Possession of such an object was too great a burden for him, even though he had smote many an opponent; this power was beyond his comprehension and knowledge. He gladly relinquished it.

With deliberate care Juliana put the orb into a velvet pouch and tightened the drawstrings. Then she tied it to a loop on her waistband. Guillem could see the enticing curve of her slender figure through the thin gown she wore beneath her cloak. He shook his head to dispel his wandering thoughts—once again Juliana's presence had him lusting for her. The witch was not the only one with power.

"Your majesty. May I request an escort for my daughter and I? We will leave at morning's break."

"My dear, Elviva, without your assistance we would be at the mercy of Malgraf this very eve. Your wish is my command."

"Sire, I will volunteer to escort Elviva and Juliana—my tale is told and I must travel on the morrow."

"You are quick to offer your services, Guillem. I know you will certainly be a very capable escort and will take extra care, I am sure, of your charges."

Guillem could not help noticing the glint in his sovereign's eye and the small curve of his lip in amusement. His secret infatuation was not lost on the other man.

"We are honored to have such a valiant escort, my lord. Our previous trepidation about our journey has diminished considerably knowing you will accompany us."

Guillem bowed his head at Elviva but his eyes stayed on Juliana's face. Her smile captivated him.

"As recompense for your part in freeing us of Malgraf, I here now honor Elviva, Juliana, and Guillem with the freedom of my lands and payment in gold coin."

The king turned and beckoned three serfs forward each carried a brocade pouch and held them out toward the honored guests. As Guillem took possession of the bag he was surprised at its weight.

"My lord, the accolade you bestow is humbling. In return, I would like to present you and Queen Rebecca with a gift."

"My dear, Guillem, without your assistance in this matter we would be at Malgraf's mercy, that is gift enough."

"Sire, it would honor me if you accepted it."

With a quickly raised hand Guillem signaled to Archie who came running into the hall carrying Guillem's saddlebags.

"Thank you, Archie."

Guillem reached inside and retrieved an ornately decorated box. As he offered it to the king he opened the lid. Nestled on a silken cloth was a bracelet of blue beads.

"The box is made from an ancient oak said to have stood for over a century, the beads have protection powers within them."

"Guillem, are these items not from your story? Do they contain black magic?"

"They are certainly not evil, sire, while in my possession I have suffered no ill. The beads would look all the more beautiful adorning the queen's arm instead of hidden within this box."

"How did you come in possession of these things?"

"That is the strange thing, my lord; I was given them by an elderly seer not three days prior to my dream of Malgraf. He was insistent I take them saying I would be in need of their protection."

"Very strange; indeed, there are forces at work here beyond our understanding but, I for one, am very happy we are the beneficiaries. Thank you, Guillem, for such fascinating objects, I will surely present the beads to Rebecca."

"Your majesty, I may be able to explain."

The king and Guillem turned to Juliana at her statement.

"Please do, Juliana."

"All evil forces are balanced by good ones, sire. The seer would certainly have known of Malgraf's plan and so would have ensured Guillem was protected."

"How can this be, Juliana, when even Guillem was not privy to his part?"

"Sire, not all things are obvious or of the practical world. Lest I say the protection worked and we are now free…"

Elviva's hand touched her granddaughter's and Juliana ceased speaking.

"Majesty, it would not do to speak of these things too freely. Our freedom has been won and we must be thankful."

"As you wish, Elviva. Now we shall retire, an early departure awaits you. Thank you all, again for releasing us from such wickedness."

With deep bows exchanged, the king left the great hall. Guillem turned to Juliana and Elviva.

"Best we follow the king's example—we have a long journey before us on the morrow."

"We shall need our rest that is for sure, Guillem. Goodnight."

Juliana cradled her grandmother's elbow in her palm and turned to the great doors. Guillem watched, yearning to follow her; sleep would be a long time coming with thoughts of her soft skin and dark eyes. As the two women broached the doorway, Juliana turned, nodded slightly and smiled. Guillem's heart leapt. *Such a simple gesture but she has me entranced.*

Chapter Eight

In his chamber, Guillem lay down watching the candlelight flicker on the stone wall. Images of Juliana appeared—her long dark hair flowing and her eyes, so dark but gentle. He succumbed to sleep with a smile on his face.

A caress on his cheek made him turn on his pillow—Juliana lay beside him—a truly pleasant dream. A kiss upon his lips—its sweetness incomparable—and it felt so real.

"I have tried to resist you, Guillem, but you hold my heart in your hands."

Her voice so near, saying words he dearly wished to hear echoing his own thoughts exactly. Another kiss, its passion unmistakable, he never wanted to wake from this particular dream.

"Will you not wake, sire?"

Was his mind playing tricks on him? He was sure he felt her warm breath on his cheek. Reluctant to open his eyes and lose the precious dream, his curiosity took priority. He blinked several times at the sight of Juliana's face so close to his. Such a dream he had never before experienced.

"I am real, sire, not a figment of your slumber."

Guillem stroked her face with the tips of his fingers, relishing its softness.

"Not a dream?"

"No, sire, not a dream, I come to you freely. Willing to accept whatever you shall bestow."

"Juliana, it is I who must accept your wishes. Never have I been so entranced or experienced such wanting. I am at your command forever more."

She answered with a kiss, its sweet gentleness made Guillem dizzy and fierce with wanting. In response, he wrapped her small frame against his muscular one. With deliberate slowness Guillem made love to Juliana. Her cries of delight further excited him. It was not until the dawn light broke through the window did they realize the extent of their passion.

"We are without rest this day, but I will not feel its effects such is the intensity of my love."

"Sire, you speak of love?"

"Yes, Juliana, it is now I understand what I feel for you. I have never felt this strength of emotion before… you have my mind, body and soul in your hands."

"Sire…"

"Please, do not address me so again, sweet Juliana. You must call me by my given name, Guillem."

"Sire, I am but a lowly maid whose infatuation would not let me rest. I do not need or require you to falsify your affections for me. I came to you willingly."

"Juliana, my feelings for you are far from false. Never before have I wanted a maid with such intensity or, indeed, fervor. I am stating my love for you as the truth, not some flippant excuse for your compliance."

Juliana's cheeks flushed red at Guillem's words. He laughed softly at her unease and placed a gentle kiss on her cheek.

"Sire…Guillem, you honor me. I know not what to say."

"Promise me you will allow me to love you, gentle Juliana. I have never known such all consuming adoration before—I wish to remain yours forever."

Before Juliana could answer him, Guillem kissed her mouth—as the sun rose over the far distant mountains so did their heat.

Elderly eyes watched from the slightly opened door.

"It is done…our journey can begin."

Elviva nodded to herself, shut the door with a gentle click and made her way back to her chamber. She would wait for Juliana to return. With their joining the task ahead would be easier to accomplish.

Chapter Nine

Surreptitiously, Guillem looked both ways along the corridor to ensure there were no witnesses' to Juliana's departure from his chamber. She had been adamant that their bond should remain a secret from the king's court. Wanting only to please, Guillem did as she bade.

"Go now, my sweet maid, I follow at a discreet distance."

Juliana placed a soft kiss on his lips then swiftly made her way to her grandmother's chamber. Her smile was difficult to disguise.

"Eldenma, are you awake?"

"Yes, my child, is the deed done?"

"As you wished, he is as captivated as you predicted."

"Good then we shall succeed in our endeavor. I have made up more potions for the journey. Make sure you have it upon your person at all times, Juliana. He must be under your spell constantly."

Juliana nodded her assent, took the small vial her grandmother offered and fastened it to her belt. With practiced ease Juliana packed their meager belongings and then assisted her elderly companion to the courtyard. Her heart skipped a beat as she saw Guillem; her feelings for him were true. She watched as he instructed several serfs on loading the rear of the cart with provisions made up of kegs and hessian wrapped parcels. At the sound of the king's voice her trance-like stare broke.

"Take great care of these two fine ladies, Guillem, their services to my realm were just as vital as yours."

"You have my word, your majesty. I shall protect them with my life."

Once Elviva and Juliana were settled onto their cart, Guillem positioned his horse beside it. With a final wave to the king and queen, and numerous onlookers, the trio headed out over the drawbridge towards the mountain range.

"Be certain to tell me if you need to rest, Elviva, the trails can be unforgiving."

"Thank you, Guillem, although I have travelled a great deal in my time

I have found my old bones are prone to complaining these last few years."

"We can pace our journey to accommodate, I am sure."

Elviva gave him a quick nod then laid her head on Juliana's shoulder. Instantly, she slept.

"I have never seen someone fall to slumber so quickly, Juliana."

"My Eldenma rests when she can, Guillem, it is not unusual for her to remain awake for many days and nights but when she sleeps it is a very deep sleep."

"We shall be able to talk freely then?"

"I am quite sure she is oblivious to her surroundings."

"May I ask how you came to call her Eldenma?"

"It is quite a story, if you can bear the telling, you a troubadour and all."

"I would delight in having a story told to me for a change. Pray, do tell."

"Eldenma is the descendant of a long line of women elders, who have special wisdom. It cannot be learned or read but is passed from mother through her daughter in the birthing, and misses a generation to be revealed in the granddaughter."

"How can that be, Juliana?"

"It is a secret I cannot divulge to you or anyone, Guillem. With the passing of an Eldenma another takes her place immediately. It has been that way for generations."

"So the name is for her position not her relation to you?"

"Yes, that is so. When Eldenma comes to her end I am to carry on in her stead."

"You… Juliana?"

"It is my path, one I have known all my life."

"What of us? I imagined we would have a life together once your task was completed."

"It is not forbidden for me to have a…"

Juliana stopped and lowered her head, unable to say the words she dearly wanted to say.

"Juliana, did I not make my feelings clear? I shall make you my wife, that, I promise you."

Juliana's hand clasped over her mouth as tears rolled down her cheeks—tears of joy at his words.

"I did not intend to make you cry, gentle Juliana."

"These are tears of happiness I assure you, Guillem. My heart is filled with delight at your words."

"As is mine that you accept my proposal even though I am not on bended knee before you."

"There will be time enough for the formalities, Guillem, but firstly we must fulfill a duty."

Elviva moaned in her sleep before opening her old yellowed eyes. She turned to see the castle quite diminished in the distance.

"You have made good time while I was sleeping. I have need to stop, if I may."

"Of course, Elviva, wait a moment, I will assist you."

Guillem tied his mount's reins to the cart and walked around to the far side. With the utmost gentleness he lifted Elviva from her seat and placed her on the dry earth.

"Thank you, kind sir, for your care and attentiveness. Please excuse me for a moment or two."

"My pleasure, Elviva. I shall make a fire so we can rest a while. The horses are in need of water, I am sure."

Guillem collected firewood and set the kindling alight as Juliana busied herself breaking bread and slicing dried meat. Elviva reappeared from the trees hobbling slightly.

"Eldenma, what happened?"

"I slipped on a root, tis nothing, Juliana, do not worry so."

"Let me see. Come, sit beside me."

Juliana revealed Elviva's ankle to find it already swollen. At her touch her grandmother gasped.

"I will make a poultice, you must stay still."

"But I…"

"I will be but a moment, Eldenma, there will be herbs a plenty for me to pick."

"May I help, Juliana?"

"Can you make sure she keeps her foot still, I will be back shortly?"

"Of course. Do not venture too far and call out so I may know your whereabouts. There may be animals lurking. Have you a dagger?"

"Yes, I do but I am sure most beasts will be slumbering in the heat of the day."

Guillem watched Juliana disappear further into the trees as he placed his bedroll behind Elviva.

"Forgive me my bluntness, Guillem, but you seem quite taken with my Juliana."

"Ah, I see no-one can hold a secret from you, Elviva. It is true Juliana has my heart like no other before her."

"She has waited long for a suitable match—treat her well, Guillem."

"It is my heartfelt wish to always make her happy and to keep her safe."

"Good…remember your words and your pledge."

Guillem frowned slightly at the inference in Elviva's words. *Did she have knowledge of a future dilemma?* Juliana's appearance at the tree line thwarted his opportunity to inquire further.

"Eldenma, I have found the herbs needed for the poultice. Has Guillem taken good care of you in my absence?"

"I could not want for a better minder, Juliana. The water is boiling and ready for you to infuse the leaves."

Guillem watched as Juliana tore leaves from various sticks and stems and dropped them into the bubbling cauldron. A sweet aroma was soon released. With great care, Juliana made a pad of the sodden leaves on a strip of cloth and wrapped it around Elviva's ankle.

"Lay still, Eldenma, so the healing can begin."

The trio sat in companionable silence, while eating their bread and meat, lost in their own thoughts. Guillem puzzled over Elviva's statement; Juliana worried over the task ahead; Elviva was concerned she would not make their destination.

Their brief respite refreshed in body, if not mind, and once again they continued toward the mountains. Guillem rode beside the cart happy to engage Juliana in relaying tales of his far away travels and battles. She asked many questions endearing her to him even more. Elviva seemed to sleep constantly when in the wagon and for this Guillem was grateful, leaving him free to speak to Juliana, uninterrupted. In the shadows of the magnificent mountains, Elviva stirred, sat upright and declared.

"Juliana head for the darkened oak in the distance, can you see it, girl?"

"Yes, its branches are twisted and bare."

"A thunderbolt struck it many moons ago, my child. Guillem be alert these foothills are populated with wolves."

"I pledged to protect and that I shall, Elviva, do not fear."

As Juliana drew the horses to a stop in front of the strange twisted tree a howl echoed against the rock face. Immediately, Guillem had his sword drawn, searching the low bushes with a practiced eye.

"A lone wolf I determine foraging but we cannot idle here for long for, he may summon his pack to join him."

"I will be but a few moments, Guillem, keep lookout while Juliana and I attend to business here."

"What sort of business can one have at an old tree?"

"That does not concern you, Guillem, just keep us safe."

Guillem frowned but did as he was instructed on Juliana's slight nod. The two women walked to the tree and crouched down at its base. He turned a complete circle seeking the undergrowth and when he looked back at the tree there was no sign of Juliana or Elviva. Panic gripped his heart. *Where could they have gone so suddenly and so quietly? Surely an animal could not have dragged them away without a sound?* He stepped toward the tree brandishing his sword, ready for battle with whatever might be ahead. There he saw a deep hollow within the tree and the flicker of a candle.

"Do not venture further, Guillem, we have almost completed our task."

Guillem reacted as he would with any firm command and stood his ground facing away from the tree. A gentle tap on his shoulder turned him to look into Juliana's sweet face.

"You keep your word, Guillem, that is a favorable trait."

"It is a point of honor to do so."

"Find us a safe haven for the night, Guillem, tomorrow will see us at our destination."

"As you direct, Elviva."

Not far from the ancient oak, Guillem found a perfect camp for their night's stay. With rock faces on three sides, its entrance was a narrow path bordered by large boulders. Any attack would come from the narrow access easily defended. Securing the horses and placing the wagon across the entrance for added security Guillem was pleased to see the flickering of flame and smell the welcome aroma of meat when he had completed his duties.

"You have certainly created a safe place to dwell, Guillem. Come, we shall eat."

Juliana held out a wooden bowl filled with steaming broth and a large chunk of bread. He relished the thick soup heavy with meat and vegetables and marveled at the fresh bread.

"How is it you can make such a feast in so little time, Juliana?"

"It is a craft handed down from my mother. Eat heartedly—there is plenty more."

Elviva sucked slowly on pieces of bread dipped in her broth while Guillem and Juliana sipped from their bowls. Wrapped in blankets against the evening chill they sat around the fire until the moon was high. Guillem's bedroll was on one side of the campfire and the two women on the other; sleep came quickly to all.

A rustling came from underneath the wagon as a small clawed animal crawled toward the humans. Its red eyes glinted, mimicking the embers. With deliberate stealth, it approached the older one, as instructed. Its forked tongue flicked in and out of its mouth constantly, much like a snake tasting its prey. One claw reached to grasp the woman's hand but was quickly severed by Guillem's blade. The creature squealed in agony then went silent as another strike cut it in half. Guillem kicked the remains away from Elviva who stared at him wide eyed.

"Guillem, how is it you were aware of the beast?"

"With years of combat experience, I am attuned to my surroundings, Juliana. This animal's approach was certainly not silent; the crackling of leaves beneath gave away its presence."

"I am very grateful you are with us, Guillem, until I heard your blade strike I was totally unaware."

"You speak the truth, child, my old ears did not hear a thing. It is fortunate we have the great Guillem Ruet to safe guard us."

"The beast was not something of this world, Elviva. Can Malgraf's familiars still be a threat?"

"You are a shrewd man, Guillem, indeed there are things left undone."

"So our journey has an ultimate goal?"

"Indeed, to purge the witch's remaining beasts from this world forever. To leave even an ounce of her essence would be too dangerous."

"Why did you keep your mission a secret from me? My loyalty to the king could not be in question surely?"

"No, Guillem, not your loyalty in any way; however, we are working for more than just the king—it is his realm that needs protecting. Our true purpose required a certain amount of secrecy from the king's court."

"Why such measures, Elviva?"

"There may be Malgraf sympathizers within the court that if left to their devices will regain power and release Malgraf from her imprisonment. That is why we had to depart so swiftly."

"I shall continue to protect you and Juliana for as long as you require my services, Elviva, for now we should try to rest before the sun rises."

"Our journey's end is almost upon us, rest well Guillem, you shall need your strength."

Elviva's soft laugh puzzled Guillem but he dismissed it as an old woman's fancy and returned to his discarded blankets. Juliana smiled as he blew her a kiss before closing his eyes. Birdsong awoke the trio early and after a quick breakfast they headed westward for a valley identified by the wise one, its distinctive jagged peak less than a morning's ride. Juliana and Guillem helped Elviva into the wagon as her ankle was paining her in the damp morning air. Once she was settled Juliana applied a poultice then wrapped her in a thick woolen blanket. Ready at last, they set off again.

Chapter Ten

As the peak grew larger in their view Elviva sat straighter and began chanting under her breath. The constant murmuring unnerved Guillem. *Did the old one know of something ahead that he should be made aware of?*

"Elviva, what lays ahead of us that has you so busy?"

"Shhh...Guillem, do not break her concentration. Eldenma has work to do before we reach the cavern."

"Cavern... what cavern?"

"Please, Guillem, be patient. I shall explain everything all in good time. Can you trust me?"

"I trust you with my life, Juliana; I will do as you wish. However, at the first sign of danger I will counter with force."

"That is all I ask, Guillem."

Elviva looked up and pointed to a dirt track nearly indistinguishable from the surrounding ground.

"There is our path, we must walk from here. Help me down, kind sir."

"I fear walking on your ankle will lead to further injury, Elviva, shall we carry you?"

"I will manage, dear girl, your poultice has helped a great deal. It was only the cold air that had it aching earlier."

Juliana held Elviva's arm to allow the older woman to lean on her as they trekked along the path. Guillem cleared overhanging branches and encroaching bushes with ease as they made their way up a steady slope. Ahead the rock face came into view and the darkness of a cave entrance.

"Will you wait a few moments, Guillem, Juliana will enter with me. Once we are ready we shall summon you."

"Should I not go first to ensure there is no danger in the darkness?"

"This place is protected by good magic, Guillem; there is nothing to fear here. Await my call."

Guillem would rather have investigated the cave's interior before letting the women enter but he could see that Elviva was sincere in her declaration.

He watched as Elviva shuffled her way over the rock surface with Juliana at her side and disappear into blackness. He anxiously strained his ears for any untoward sounds or cries of assistance but only heard birdsong and crickets.

"You may enter, Guillem, but leave your sword and dagger—no weapons may enter this place."

Sword and dagger discarded, Guillem entered the cavern then stood for a moment so his eyes could adjust to the gloom. A soft golden light guided him deeper into the cavern's interior. He had expected a dank, cold and possibly wet earthen floored cave but was astonished to find a luscious chamber filled with heavy oak furniture and a fireplace.

"What is this place? How can this be real? Surely I am dreaming?"

"Welcome to the home of my ancestors, Guillem. Generations ago the first Eldenma created what you see before you. It is a sacred place where endings are completed and beginnings are begun."

"Come and sit by the fire with me, Guillem. We are safe here and I wish to show you something very important."

As Guillem sat beside Juliana she placed a heavy leather bound book on his lap. "This is a record of all the Eldenmas who have lived, their deeds and their legacies."

Engrossed in the images and writing before him, Guillem turned page after page with increasing worry. Each Eldenma had taken her own life willingly leaving her granddaughter to carry on in her stead.

"Elviva, you cannot be considering this action surely? Juliana you would not let your grandmother do such a thing?"

"It is our way, Guillem; the Eldenma title skips a generation. We do not question our fate for one woman can be blessed with the status while another by a trick of her birth does not have the honor."

"Is there no other way the title can be passed on?"

"The edict is very exact—this is the way it has been done for numerous generations. Elviva has always known this moment would come and that it is her duty. She does it without question."

"I cannot stand by and let her take her own life. She may be old but surely she has many moons yet."

"My darling, Guillem, it is her choice alone which date she chooses for her end, no other dictates it. We will sleep this night within our ancestor's house and on the morrow Elviva will announce her choice of day."

"I have served and fought with many men in my life, Juliana, but none have willingly chosen to end their life at their own hand. I find this incomprehensible."

"Elviva will live on within the pages of this book, Guillem; she has a fantastical tale to tell. She saved King Henry's realm from Malgraf and once she has completed the final part of her quest she will be ready for her last act."

Juliana took Guillem's hand and placed it on her breast. He looked around in trepidation—*was Elviva near?*

"Fear not, Guillem, Elviva has travelled down into the mountain for she has work to do with the confinement orb. We are quite alone and free to enjoy each other—if you wish it."

His hands and mouth answered for him—his hunger for Juliana was all absorbing. Time and time again he satisfied himself and took Juliana to pleasurable heights on the hearth rug. At last, with their sweat glowing in the firelight, they wrapped their bodies in blankets and watched the flames lap over large logs in the hearth. With sleight of hand, Juliana sprinkled a little dust over Guillem's head and soon he fell into a deep sleep.

With great care she stood and slipped into a sheer gown. From a box on the hearth she took a pair of scissors and cut several locks of hair from Guillem's head. These she placed back into the box then nicked his finger with a small blade and let the blood fill a small vial. Once it was corked it, too, went into the box and Juliana closed the lid.

"Sleep well, dear Guillem, your part will become clear on the morrow."

Juliana raised her head at the sound of shuffling. Elviva had returned.

"Is the deed done? Are you with child?"

"Yes, it is done. The child grows as we speak."

"He is a robust man, Juliana, his child will be strong. Now attend to your charms while I make the potion. You have the necessary?"

"Yes, Eldenma, his essence parts are in the carved box on the hearth. We have several hours before he wakes."

"You have done well, Juliana, you will surely surpass my deeds in your time as Eldenma."

"My future path is written, I will follow it as is my destiny."

"Fine words, my child, but you have the power to change the way you walk that path, remember that..."

Juliana embraced Elviva noticing the older woman's frail stature.

"We must make haste – the preparations will take several hours and you need to rest before the ceremony, Eldenma."

Elviva collected the box from the hearth and smiled. Soon she would be released and Juliana would be her successor, a worthy one at that. She shuffled away along a passageway to attend to her task knowing that Juliana would be intent upon her own. At a small table she placed the box down and retrieved its contents. She uncorked the vial and poured Guillem's blood into a silver chalice then she began mixing herbs to make an infusion.

Juliana had taken another passageway, which took her downward to a bubbling underground stream. The water was sweet to the taste, its power hidden in its clarity. She recovered a crystal goblet nestled on a natural shelf and scooped up the clear liquid. As she drank the cool fluid her heart beat faster, her complexion glowed and her eyes sparkled. Invigorated, she filled the goblet once again and began chanting, in a low whisper, least the echoed words reach Guillem. His time would come but she needed to prepare first.

"Font of life, bestow your gift,
Your secret I shall keep,
The burden I shall shoulder,
My destiny, yours to hold."

With great care not to spill a drop, Juliana returned to the larger cavern. After placing the goblet on a table she lay down beside Guillem once again and feigned sleep. It would be best if he woke naturally and unaware of her absence.

Elviva, meanwhile, had crafted her infusion. She poured it over oats and began to stir the mixture ensuring the special substance was completely absorbed. She would offer Guillem a bowl of steaming porridge to fortify him—he would be hungry when he awoke blissfully ignorant of the fact his sleep had been manufactured.

Slowly opening his eyes, Guillem still felt heavy with sleep; he never before had such a slumber. It was difficult to shake off the fog of unconsciousness but his view of a slumbering Juliana lying next to him made him smile. He gently traced his fingers across her cheek, *such softness.* Her lips curled into a smile before her eyes opened to gaze back at him. Yet again he was surprised at their depth of colour almost black - like no other he had ever seen before.

"You slept well, I trust, Guillem?"

"Never better, might it be the company I kept that gave me such a restful sleep?"

"Might it be the events prior to sleep that had you so tired?"

Her slight flush had him laughing. She surely spoke the truth, their lovemaking had continued for several hours. No other maid, he had enjoyed the pleasure of, could match the intensity and willingness to comply with his wishes as Juliana. She was truly a unique woman.

"Am I intruding?"

Elviva's croaky voice broke their gaze as they turned to face the old woman. She was carrying a small black cauldron from which steam rose.

"I have brought a hearty breakfast for our intrepid guardian. Please, be seated at the table, Guillem, so I may serve you."

"That is very kind, Elviva, wait let me help you with that heavy pot."

Guillem took the cast iron pot out of her weathered hands and placed it on the table. The aroma of hot oats filled his nostrils and his stomach voiced its need. Elviva put a pewter bowl in front of Guillem as he took a seat and began spooning out steaming porridge. Juliana went to a small alcove and brought back a sizable wedge of cheese and a large loaf.

"Ladies, you will join me?

"Alas, neither of us are partial to oats, Guillem, it is enough that we see you enjoy them. We have bread and cheese to sustain us."

Juliana and Elviva sat either side of Guillem. They tore off pieces from the fresh loaf and sliced the cheese thickly. They ate in silence for a while each enjoying the good food.

"Elviva, I must compliment you on your porridge, it is the best I have ever tasted. What secret ingredient do you add?"

"It is a very old recipe passed down from mother to daughter—I am not at liberty to say how it is made. However, Juliana will receive the recipe, in due course."

"I hope she will do me the honor of making it for me then in the not too distant future."

"So I trust your intentions toward my granddaughter are honorable, too?"

"Most certainly, Elviva, she is the most charming, beautiful and fascinating woman I have ever met. If she will allow me to court her I will be the happiest man alive."

"Your sincerity is heartwarming, Guillem. Knowing Juliana will be protected, after I am gone, brings me peace."

"A day, I trust, that will be many moons from now."

Guillem noticed the two women look at each other, mistaking it for agreement and fondness. With the bowl of porridge finished, he stretched and excused himself to go outside. Once he relieved himself, he attended to the horses with water and tethered them near fresh grass. As he breathed in the mountain air, he realized how light hearted he felt—a feeling he had lost long ago in the fighting of many battles, constantly seeing death all around him, grueling treks over desolate wastelands as a younger man, and the loneliness of his current profession. He had welcomed a solitary life, at first, unable to rid himself of the horrific visions that plagued him night after night and the suffocation he felt in crowds. Initially, his quick reactions had many an innocent bystander at the tip of his blade. His perceptions were altered from decades of combat, but gradually he gained a resemblance of normal behavior after a few years of solitary travel. He had come to terms with his inner beasts over time and now with the love of Juliana he could see a future worth pursuing.

Echoed words met him as he re-entered the cavern, Elviva and Juliana were huddled together beside the fireside. The small cauldron hung on a hook and its contents bubbled furiously. The aroma was pleasant but unknown to Guillem.

"What are you cooking up now, Elviva, another tasty snack for me?"

"As it happens it is something for you, Guillem. However, this mixture is for an important ritual that concerns you and Juliana."

"A ritual—what kind of ceremony are we talking of here?"

"Follow us, if you please, Guillem, I shall reveal all—once we are at the assigned position."

"You are being most mysterious, old woman, but if it is Juliana's wish, I shall comply."

"Guillem, it is my greatest wish that you join me in this rite."

"Then lead on—I shall follow."

With Juliana's hand cradling her elbow for support, Elviva lead them down a dark passageway sloping downward, deeper into the cavern's depths. Guillem lit a torch to light their way once the main cave's light diminished. The rock glistened in the flame showing them water seeping through and dripping softly onto the pathway.

"Be very careful of your footing, Eldenma, you cannot suffer a fall."

"I have you and Guillem to hold me steady, my dear. It is not much further."

A twist in the passage revealed another cavern, this one much larger and covered in numerous glistening stalagmites and stalactites in blues and greens. Glassy pools mirrored the ceiling until a single drop broke the surface sending ripples outward.

"This is magnificent; I have never seen such a place in all my travels."

"It is a special place, Guillem, known to only a few. We shall perform the rite over yonder."

Guillem followed the direction of Elviva's pointing finger. On the far side, he could make out in the dim light an altar, of sorts, carved from the rock face. He felt uneasy and stopped walking.

"What sort of ritual are you proposing, Elviva?"

"Neither you nor Juliana will come to harm, Guillem, trust my word."

Relieved, Guillem stepped forward to lift Elviva over a trickling stream whose rock edges were smooth and slippery. Once on the other side, he gently placed the elderly woman on a dry surface and held out his hand to Juliana. Her eyes met his as they radiated golden tones. His shock held him fast—*her eyes were normally of the deepest brown to almost black, how could they change so?*

"Do not fear, my love, I will only be altered for a while – it is nothing to fear."

"What is this…what haven't you told me?"

"Come, I will show you."

Chapter Eleven

Juliana took Guillem's hand and led him to the altar. Upon it were a couple of jewel encrusted goblets and a pewter dish also adorned with jewels. As they approached, Juliana raised her hand and dozens of candles lit.

"What devilment is this? Am I at the mercy of witchcraft?"

"Certainly not devilment, my love, but it is magic of sorts – a good magic, unlike that of Malgraf and her dark arts."

"Have I been bewitched, my senses altered and twisted for some purpose I would not willingly partake?"

"Absolutely not… you are at liberty to make choices and decisions."

"Then tell me the truth, Juliana, why am I here?"

"If you are willing, tonight you and I will be united, much like a marriage, but for eternity."

Guillem's stunned silence had the two women look at each other and then back at him tensing as they awaited his answer.

"I envisaged marriage in the future, Juliana, and in truth, hoped it would be so, but I need to know exactly what this rite entails. What am I getting into?"

"As you may have ascertained, Elviva, has special powers; those powers are passed from grandmother to granddaughter, a tradition lost in time. Now is my time to become Eldenma…"

"You become an Eldenma, this very night?

"Yes, I will bear the title once the ritual is complete. It signifies my position and authority."

"And what of my part in this ceremony?"

"An Eldenma is obliged to have an consort, a protector if you will, for there will be times when my life will be threatened."

"Threatened by whom?"

"My powers can defeat demons, witches and devilment of all kinds thus, I may be hunted. You have shown great courage and resolve, traits which assure me you are the protector for me… if you agree."

"I would gladly lay down my life for you, Juliana, of that have no doubt. My reluctance comes from the unknown as the things you speak of are a mystery to me."

"Juliana, my child, in light of Guillem's sincerity it might be best to tell him of all this rite involves. My heart is certain he will consent once all the details are relayed."

"As you order, Eldenma."

Juliana bowed deeply. Guillem saw the respect Juliana held for her grandmother in that one movement. The pair obviously shared more than just the love between relations.

"Please, sit beside me, Guillem, let me explain what this particular night signifies for me and Eldenma."

As Guillem sat and faced Juliana, Elviva walked to the altar. Although her back was shielding her movements he could see her hands were busy and she softly mumbled to herself.

"Look into my eyes, Guillem, do not concern yourself with Eldenma and her tasks. There will be time enough for that part."

Once again Guillem was intrigued with the golden tone of Juliana's eyes. *How could they change so?* Seated, facing each other, Juliana took both his hands in hers and began.

"This night will see a wondrous change in all our lives, something very few people ever witness. I will become the new Eldenma."

"And what does this new title bring with it, Juliana? Have you powers such as your grandmother?"

"I was born with powers similar to Eldenma's but each Eldenma has her own particular strengths and charms. My grandmother will pass her title to me this night and begin a new journey of her own."

"Where could such an old woman travel? She is noticeably frailer than the first time I saw her. Is she ailing?"

"In a manner of speaking, yes, she is ailing though not a physical sickness but, rather, a spiritual one. Her time has come and she is impatient to complete this rite."

"Are you saying… that Elviva is dying?"

"Again, not as you understand it—yes, she will leave her present body but in time will return."

"Return? How can that be? Ashes to ashes, dust to dust—once a body loses it life surely that is the end? I have seen with my own eyes—many a man die and none have ever returned."

"That is true for most men and women, but my grandmother and I are from a different line, a special line. Passing from one life to another; generation after generation. I have lived before as has Eldenma—re-birthing time and again."

Guillem heard the words Juliana said but could not comprehend them. He was silent for a time gazing at her beautiful face to see if she was sincere. Not once did she turn away or break their eye contact. *If her words are true is she young or old?*

Juliana tried to make sense of the emotions shown on Guillem's face. She understood how strange it all must seem. He was a practical man at heart and showed great courage destroying Malgraf but his understanding of such powers was obviously limited. He used his fearlessness to overcome. With great gentleness, she placed a hand on his cheek.

"Do you trust me, Guillem?"

"With all my heart, Juliana but can you understand my puzzlement?"

"Yes, of course, I can. Tonight, we shall be joined together eternally - in this life and the ones in the future. You may visualize it as a marriage but it is more than that as we are mystical soul mates. You will be my guardian and, I, your mistress. However, ultimately it must be your decision this night as I am forbidden to force or coerce you."

Guillem hid a smile at the thought of this delicate woman even trying to force him into anything let alone force.

"So how does this eternal link come to be?"

"Eldenma will perform a ritual, our blood will be mixed and our breath combined."

"Juliana, I have never known such depth of feeling until I met you—if I can keep you near, without end, I am happy to do so."

Juliana's arms embraced his neck and her lips pushed against his, passionately. His body responded but Elviva's voice cut their moment short.

"He agreed then?"

"Yes, Eldenma, Guillem will stand by my side."

"Good, then come to the altar the two of you, time is passing. Time I cannot waste."

Hands tightly gripped together they approached the old woman.

"Guillem stand on my left and face Juliana. My child, to my right and take this goblet."

The goblet held a milky substance but before Guillem could ask its contents Elviva withdrew a dagger from the folds in her cloak. Without a word Juliana held out her hand and watched unflinching as Elviva cut a line along her left ring finger. The old woman turned to Guillem and nodded toward his hand. He mimicked Juliana's movements and saw an identical line cut into his ring finger. Elviva then placed their hands palm to palm and began to chant.

"Blood on blood
Soul with soul
Bind through time
Eternal bond
Never to break."

Guillem felt a tingle go through his hand and up his arm then spread throughout his body. It was invigorating. As he looked up, he was startled to see Juliana's eyes glowing gold, and Elviva's the same. He tried to pull his hand away but it was stuck fast to Juliana's. She shook her head slightly and Guillem stood still. *Let what may be happen.*

"Sup from the goblet, Juliana, then pass it to Guillem, right hand to right hand. Do not break the blood bond."

Juliana did as she was asked then passed the cup to Guillem, the cool liquid had a pleasant aroma and taste but was thick like syrup. The fluid flowed, and the tingling increased, spreading through his body. He felt perceptively stronger and vigorous.

"What is this draft we drink, Elviva? Its effects are immediate."

"An elixir to fortify your body, Guillem. So you are ready for the passage you will take."

"Passage…?"

"Trust me, Guillem, you will not come to harm, in fact, you will know verve unlike any you have ever known even as a youth. It will sustain you."

Guillem nodded his ascent and awaited the next part of the ritual. So far he had not suffered in any great way—even the cut on his finger seemed dulled.

"You may release each other's hands now. Stand side by side and face the altar. The objects I ask you to hold are to be handled with great care and not released."

Elviva turned back to the altar, picked up two crystals, one golden the other red and placed them into Juliana's hands. With another turn she collected two more crystals, one ebony in colour and one dark green and placed them in Guillem's outstretched hands.

"Please, bow your heads and repeat my words. Fear not when the stones vibrate and grow warm, it is meant to be."

Elviva touched Guillem's furrowed brow with spindly fingers, calmness washed through him. Satisfied the two were ready, Elviva began to chant.

"Time unbind, circle back and forth
Souls unite unbroken
Forever tied mistress and guardian
Powers strong and undefeated."

The crystals glowed and warmed to the touch, Guillem looked to Juliana for direction.

"Hold them fast, Guillem, you will experience a spinning sensation but it is the way through."

Before Guillem could ask another question, the walls of the cave began to turn, faster and faster they went but he was still within them. A very disorientating sensation to be sure but Juliana was there by his side, smiling. He mimicked her movements when she raised her clasped hands and touched the stones to his. Light issued from the crystals in multi coloured threads swathing Juliana and Guillem in a cloak and obscuring the cavern. Guillem felt as if he were floating and was about to utter his feelings when Juliana's body lifted several feet above him. Astonished Guillem looked downward to see they were indeed floating above the rocks below.

"Juliana, what is this?"

"Do not fret, Guillem, our passage has begun. Soon we will be united in body and spirit."

Guillem was lost for words. *How could they fly like birds?* As he looked up he was further astounded to see not the cavern ceiling dominated with stalactites but a whirling vortex of gold, ebony, green and red. If not for Juliana's calm, smiling face, he would have fought this uncertainty. Although how he would fight this apparition was in doubt.

At the apex, Juliana opened her arms and embraced Guillem, whispering as she did.

"Guillem, my sentinel, my love, naught can divide us from this moment on. We are one—to travel the eons together."

Within her embrace the spinning sensation slowed, then ceased. Guillem felt the rock beneath his feet and looked around to see the altar and cavern walls unchanged. However, Elviva was nowhere in sight.

"Has the ritual exhausted, Elviva, Juliana?"

"Elviva has gone forth on a journey of her own, Guillem. She is not of this world any longer."

"She's dead?"

"The body she inhabited has left this earthly realm but her spirit lives in another. Fear not, Guillem, she is in a place of joy—her rightful place."

"You speak without any hint of sadness, Juliana; I am puzzled at your nonchalance of your grandmother's passing. Even though I had not known her any great length of time, she struck me as a wise and interesting woman."

"Guillem, now is not the time—we must complete the ritual."

"There is more?"

"The crystals must be reformed and placed in their trove. Then, we will have time to talk."

Guillem had not noticed until that moment that the crystals were soft and pliable in his hands totally unlike hard stones. His bewildered look had Juliana laughing as she took the soft forms from him and placed them on a pewter plate upon the altar. As she chanted strange words and sprinkled a grainy powder over the plaint forms Guillem could see them change. Within moments the crystals were angled hard forms once again. Juliana placed them in an ornate carved box, closed the lid and placed her hands upon it.

"Seal and guard
Treasurers within
Never unlock
Until she comes
My successor of time."

Chapter Twelve

"Juliana, will you tell me now of our future together?"

"Yes, Guillem, I will after we drink and eat. Are you not in need of sustenance?"

His hunger took him by surprise at her words. Guillem was indeed parched and his stomach made an audible grumble to confirm his appetite.

"Strange that I can be so famished after such a short time."

"Our joining took a day, Guillem, within the vortex time has no meaning. The special porridge Eldenma made gave you sustenance for the journey."

Juliana laughed gently at Guillem's obvious shock and kissed his cheek.

"A whole day… what was in that gruel?"

"It is a special mixture of herbs and essences to fortify the body."

"It surely would have made many arduous treks and battles the easier for me and the men I served with, that's for sure. I had no idea we had been within the spinning web that long."

"Eldenma certainly had great skill in preparing potions—many she taught me as a young child."

"I trust you can replicate that particular one—it would prove very useful in many applications."

Juliana was in no doubt as to Guillem's thinly disguised meaning. She turned and made her way to the rear of the cavern, smiling. He would satisfy her for many moons.

Soon the aroma of meat stew pervaded the cave. Guillem came to stand beside Juliana as she stirred the thick liquid. The horses had also been in need of water and feed so Guillem had busied himself with their needs while Juliana cooked.

"Come, sit Guillem, a hearty meal with plenty of ale will satisfy you."

Seated at the table, they consumed the meal in silence, sating their appetites steadily. Guillem's tankard was emptied and refilled numerous times but Juliana's not so many. She wanted her wits about her for later.

With the meal finished they went to sit nearer the fireplace and sighed with contentment. It was not long before Guillem's eyes began to close.

"Let us retire to bed, Guillem; we will be much more comfortable there."

"I must apologize with a full belly and plenty of ale supped I am overcome with tiredness. Please, forgive me."

"There is nothing to forgive, Guillem; you have endured a great deal in the past few days—it is to be expected. Come, lay with me."

Naked bodies entwined, slumber came quickly. However, just before the sun began its climb upward Juliana woke, slipped from the bed, and retrieved a vial from the altar. She gently uncorked it and sipped a little of the contents then moistened Guillem's lips with the rest. He stirred in his sleep and licked his lips.

"Immortality is yours as well as mine now, my dear, Guillem, it is a burden but also a joy. Take heart that we will be together for eternity."

Chapter Thirteen

Guillem woke to Juliana's soft kisses on his cheek, the most pleasant of awakenings. One he would relish for many long years.

"Good morning, my love, I trust you are well rested?"

"I am rested and full of vigor, my gentle Juliana."

As Guillem's hands caressed her shoulders, Juliana halted them in their downward motion.

"I have something to tell you, Guillem, something I hope will fill you with joy."

"You have proved to be my joy, Juliana, I am at a lost as to what else you could tell me that would make me happier."

"Guillem, as you have now comprehended, our bond is eternal but we also have a link to the future."

"You are speaking in riddles, Juliana, if we live forever we will know the future."

"We will not always exist in this realm, my love."

She gently laughed at Guillem's shocked face; he was stunned into silence.

"Fear not…"

"I do not fear, Juliana, the events of the past few days have diminished my preconceptions. What more can there be?"

"I am with child—a blessing for us both—I hope you agree?"

"Pregnant so soon—are you sure?"

"Very sure, my love, are you not pleased?'

"Shocked, surprised, but…"

Juliana looked into Guillem's eyes uncertainty plaguing her thoughts *Maybe she should have kept her secret a little longer?* Guillem's hands clasped hers tightly and a slow smile creased his face.

"Forgive me for my stunned silence, Juliana, I had not expected to find an all consuming love at thirty years old, let alone, become a father. I have to admit I am feeling overwhelmed but excited at the same time."

"So you are happy with my news?"

"Yes, in fact, I am feeling quite elated."

Juliana threw her arms around Guillem's neck and kissed him passionately. Their heat rose quickly but suddenly Guillem stopped.

"You are with child, Juliana, we cannot."

"Do not worry, my love, no harm will come to me or the baby. Satisfy me now—my yearning is heightened."

Guillem did not hesitate to comply with Juliana's request. His love for this extraordinary woman knew no bounds, figuratively and literally. He felt sure their life together would be full of excitement and adventures. Now, he would also be a father and all that would bring. He had never known such happiness—their lives stretched before them—he would treasure this gift for all time.

Epilogue

Juliana held her granddaughter in her arms; it was a bitter sweet moment. The child was a delight but also her replacement. A sure indication that the life she had enjoyed with Guillem in this earthly realm would come to an end. She knew it was the order of things for the Eldenma line but this particular life had been so extraordinary she was less inclined to leave it. Once they relinquished themselves in the ritual, the new Eldenma would take her place and she and Guillem would begin another type of existence in a spiritual realm.

"Eldenma, you are crying. Are you displeased with my daughter?"

"Of course, not my darling child, these are tears of happiness. Come, let us present your beautiful baby to the men."

Juliana walked side by side with her daughter, Celeste, through the passageway to the large cavern. Guillem and Michael stood expectantly at the appearance of their lovers.

"Come and meet, Maralynn, the most delightful little baby I have ever seen apart from my own darling, Celeste, of course."

The four adults crowded around the infant. At that precise moment, Maralynn opened her golden eyes—there was such intensity in them her observers were taken aback at the obvious power this new little being held. A thin thread of cyan mist floated above the happy group … unobserved Maralynn's reign as Eldenma would be fraught with challenges but her exceptional power would ultimately overcome.

We trust you enjoyed Guillem's adventures and thank you for purchasing this novella. A sequel following Celeste's journey will follow in 2018. An announcement will be made on the publisher's website www.dreamwritepublishing.ca

Mandy Eve-Barnett

To give you a glimpse into the author—she is a fairly new Canadian resident, who has a wealth of experiences to draw from for her writing. She has lived in South Africa, England and Canada and the uniqueness of each continent has left its essence within her. An avid reader her whole life, it wasn't until she joined a local writing group, the Writers Foundation of Strathcona County, that the writing 'bug' gripped her. Now Mandy Eve-Barnett writes with an all-encompassing passion and is deeply involved with the foundation and its members. Writing in various genres, Mandy has published four books (as at 2017), as well as in anthologies, on numerous web sites, and in the local newspaper. She has successfully completed many National Novel Writing Month challenges.

You can find her blog at www.mandyevebarnett.com and follow her on Twitter @mandyevebarnett.

(Author photo by Mario Maier Photography)

Made in the USA
Middletown, DE
09 August 2021